# BLOC TRILOGY

## BOOK TWO

### PAIGE TAYLOR

To Tsya,

Enjoy your read!

*Paige Taylor*

ISBN: 978-1-962825-99-3

MUSKOKA
Authors Association

# Also by Paige Taylor

**Blood Blade Trilogy:**

Secrets Wrought in Blood

Hearts Woven in War

Praise for

# Hearts Woven in War

"Paige Taylor has outdone herself with this sequel in the Blood Blade trilogy! Buckle up as you embark on this compelling roller coaster of a journey. Taylor deftly hits all the right notes, with passion, adventure, rich characters, knuckle-biting tension, and the universal battle of good vs evil beautifully coalescing into a page-turner that's sure to delight audiences of all ages!"

– Cindy Watson, award-winning and best-selling author of *The Art of Feminine Negotiation* and *Out of Darkness*.

"Taylor has done it again! After reading her amazing debut novel, the sequel exceeded my expectations, sending me on another, unforgettable journey. Don't miss the rise of this up-and-coming superstar in the fantasy genre."

– Richard H. Stephens, author of the Soul Forge Universe

# TABLE OF CONTENTS

# Playlist

Our Song - Anne-Marie & Nial Horan

IDGAF - Dua Lipa

You Are The Reason - Calum Scott

Lose Somebody - Kygo & One Republic

Used To - Sandro Cavazza

Hurts 2B Human - P!nk feat. Khalid

Wolves - Selena Gomez & Marshmello

Paradise - MEDUZA

Better Man - Virginia to Vegas

If I Don't Laugh, I'll Cry - Frawley

The Night We Met - Lord Huron

Surrender - Natalie Taylor

Ghost of You - 5 Seconds of Summer

Little Lion man - Mumford & Sons

# PART ONE

## BROKEN BONDS

# ONE

## THALIA

Rain.

The cruel sting of rain.

Cold and pure, it carves emblems into my flesh, like ancient symbols to stone. Permanent and unforgivable. Bitter and painful, the droplets linger, soaking through my skin, straight to the bone.

I feel my limbs trembling, but it is distant. Like I am a ghost of myself, waiting in the blissful darkness for a sign of hope, of light, as my body quivers against the cold.

But there is darkness. Only darkness. A sheet of black before my eyes, blocking all else out. I fight against it: but I am incapable of movement and lost in a haze of nothingness. Yet there is something beyond the eternal shadows, something I cannot reach. Something I strive to reach.

A voice.

There is a voice.

Far away and muffled. I cannot decipher the words nor whom the voice belongs to, but I struggle towards them, battling my unresponsive body as I am weighed down in the blackness.

My eyes flicker.

The world around me is blurry, meshed together and shrouded by a stubborn grey mist that only relents when I begin to blink, forcing it to recede slowly. A face appears.

Sharp, defined jaw and pointed ears. Pale blonde hair falls over their shoulders and frames their face, highlighting their piercing eyes.

Silver eyes.

*Killian.*

I jolt upright, propping myself onto my shoulders to see him better. The world whips in a furious circle, and I inhale sharply, too weak to hold myself up. I drop back into the gravelly soil, sharp stones digging into my back. There is a vicious pounding and heaviness in my skull, and I raise my hands, pressing them against the side of my head in an attempt to vanquish the pain. My features curve into a wince.

"Hey! Careful," Killian's tone is calm, and I feel a swell of security wash over me at the familiar voice. His calloused fingers close around my wrists, gently pulling them away from my face. "Easy, Thalia."

The pounding intensifies, and I wonder if my head shall explode. When I am confident it shall not, I open my eyes slowly, quickly regretting it. The world spins violently, a mixture of green leaves and brown trunks framing a grey sky.

"Here."

There is a shuffling from my side, the faint click of a buckle, opened, then closed. I notice that my cloak has been laid over me, a temporary blanket. Killian holds his waterskin out.

I prop myself onto my elbows once more, slower this time as I brace myself against the wave of dizziness. Nausea settles in the pit of my

11

stomach, and I bite my lip to keep from vomiting.

"You are awake," a female voice echoes.

Painfully, my eyes flicker to Aliya. She kneels beside Alistar, a bloodied cloth in one hand, a makeshift bandage in the other. Her lips are curved into a relieved grin as she brings herself to stand.

"I—" My hand flies to my throat, caught off guard by the croak in my voice. It is sore from my silence and lack of water.

"You need to drink."

Gently, Killian presses his waterskin into my hands. I take it gratefully, grimacing as I shuffle backwards and settle against an oak tree. I flip the cap open, taking a sip of the cool water. It soothes my parched throat, momentarily calming the hammering in my head.

I pass it back to him, nodding my appreciation.

"Thank you."

"Anything, Thalia. You do not have to thank me." I watch as he drops his waterskin onto the ground beside him, then shifts his position so that his back rests against the tree, and he is settled beside me, one leg drawn up to his chest, head tipped back against the bark. He stares up at the dull sky, and I focus on the silver-blue of his eyes, on the way they flicker back and forth, examining the thick grey clouds.

"Glad to see you are well," Alistar calls, yet his tone lacks humour. His head is tilted, and he attempts to smile, yet it is more akin to a grimace.

I raise my eyebrows in question, and his lips quirk, offering me a lopsided grin. I do not return it, my attention caught by the slit on his shin. The blood-stained fabric is parted to reveal a gruesome gash, one I am certain he acquired during our last battle.

"It seems you are doing just as well as I," I point out.

His smile slips away.

"Yes, it would seem so."

A chill runs down my spine, and I grasp the edge of my cloak, pulling it closer and relishing its warmth.

Beyond the trees, a twig snaps, and I direct my attention upon Thorne. He emerges from the brush, hand curled around the ears of a dead rabbit, which dangles in the air. His eyes dart to me, and he halts, surveying me. He blinks once, then bows his head in silence, offering me nothing more than stone-faced acknowledgement. Continuing, he drops down upon a crumbling log.

Leaves rustle beside me, crunching as Killian shifts his weight. I roll my head to the side, finding him watching me, his body angled slightly to the side so that he may see me better. I shift, my features curving into a wince as I take up the same position as him. I study him. His straight, honey-blonde hair is damp and crusted with blood, his face splattered with it, and dirt mars his cheeks. A single cut is etched into his jaw, and his silver-blue eyes are clouded, deep bags lingering beneath them, exhaustion relentless in its hold upon him.

"How do you feel?" he asks.

I laugh, yet the gesture rattles my skull, and I grimace.

"Awful. I would not be surprised if my skull exploded, Killian."

His throat bobs as he swallows, and he tips his head back to look at the slated skies. "You are lucky to be alive. That was a powerful blow you took."

Idly, I run my thumb over the fabric of my cloak, holding it tight against me as a barrier against the cold.

"Indeed."

My lips twist into a frown, one I am quick to conceal.

There is something missing.

Something is nagging at my mind— a thought I cannot discern. I squint at the trees, wracking my brain for a clue, yet it reveals nothing. Still, I cannot vanquish the feeling, the pit in my stomach that tells me something is wrong. Something not quite right, something missing. Something crucial.

I turn back to Killian, deciding not to pursue the thought, for my mangled thoughts and exhaustion limit my thinking. I tilt my head so that I may meet his eyes.

"How do you feel?"

He rolls his head to the side, eyes locking onto mine. "I have been better."

"You were lucky to leave that fight unscathed," I say, then reach out, motioning towards the cut on his jaw. "For the most part."

He brushes his fingers over the gash; lips pulled into a thin line. "A mere cut. It is nothing compared to what you suffered."

"I am alive; that is all that matters."

He bows his head, his silence a contradiction of the thoughts portrayed within his eyes.

I wish to comfort him, yet words evade me, so instead, I turn away, pulling my damp hair over my shoulder and running my fingers through the knots, lost in thought. I scan the woods as I work to free the tangles.

Silence ensues, and after a moment, Killian brings himself to stand. He scrubs at a speck of blood on his silver pauldron, oddly intent on regaining its shine. My eyebrows knit together as I watch him carefully. The action is not unusual, but it is not Killian. His demeanour has changed. He is still the stern, strong-willed man, yet there is an undertone of anguish to his behaviour, of anxiety.

"What is bothering you?"

He grows unnaturally still, his persistent scrubbing at the dirt coming to a pause. Slowly, he lifts his head, looking ahead into the forest, expression like stone.

"Nothing, Thalia."

He does not meet my gaze when he speaks and quickly drops his hands from his pauldron as if realising his mistake. He moves to Elwis's side, searching for something in his satchel.

"Liar."

He freezes, and my heart plummets.

This is not Killian, and his anxious movements only add to the unease building in my belly, confirming my earlier fear. There is something on his mind, something he cannot ignore. Something I am missing. I lean to the side, peering around him. He offers me no acknowledgement.

"Killian," I breathe, a warning in my tone.

15

He rotates toward me, tossing the last of his berries into my lap.

"You need to eat."

I stare at the pouch, unsure of how to react. His behaviour unnerves me, and I cannot help but wonder if he feels the same sense of unease as I, that something is wrong. Subconsciously, my fingers search for Valindor's hilt, seeking reassurance in its power.

They meet nothing but damp grass.

My breath hitches, and I throw my cloak aside, rolling onto my knees and digging frantically through the rough soil. The hammering in my skull intensifies, and the corners of my vision grow blurry with the threat of falling back into unconsciousness. Nevertheless, I continue to scramble.

Valindor is not here.

*It. Is. Not. Here.*

"Thalia—"

I stumble to my feet, staggering towards Killian as wave after wave of dizziness overwhelms me, and the world tilts.

"Where is it?" I cry. Killian's hands find my elbows, steadying me.

"Valindor—"

"Thalia, calm down."

"Where is it?" I struggle against him, trying to break away from his unyielding grasp, yet his fingers have closed around my wrists, making it impossible for me to free myself. I sway, my head spinning, and he pulls me against his chest, holding me still as the panic claws at my insides.

"You need to calm down."

"*No.*" Terror prickles my skin, and my legs begin to tremble. I try to pull away from him, but he is too powerful.

"Thalia, look at me."

"Killian—" My voice cracks.

His hands fly to my face, forcing me to meet his gaze. I feel tears prick my eyes, hot and stinging, and I force them closed as the terror clamps around my heart, squeezing so painfully that I struggle to breathe.

"*Relax,*" he says gently.

I cannot.

I shove his chest, breaking free of his arms. Stumbling back, my vision is blurred by traitorous tears, and the world around me spins in a vicious circle.

"*Tell me where Valindor is, Killian.*" Despite my terror, the deadliness of my tone is unmistakable.

He stares at me for a moment, his beautiful eyes softened with pity, *regret*. It makes my stomach drop.

After a moment, he averts his gaze, body shuddering with a ragged breath. His hesitation only adds to the pit of fear in my stomach, sinking further into the depths of dread with every second that ticks by.

"I could not save you and Valindor both."

I feel my heart stutter as his words sink into my skin, poisoning my blood and infiltrating my mind and soul.

I press a trembling hand to my mouth, and my nails dig into my flesh, but I feel no pain.

"The racai retrieved Valindor."

# TWO
## THALIA

M y lips part, yet I find myself incapable of speech.

I stand utterly still, a jumble of emotions. Anger and fear and shock. They meld together, the lines of each too blurred to distinguish, and I feel myself begin to tremble. To shake with violent, uncontrollable ire.

"*They. What?*" My voice is a whisper, yet it drips with acid.

Killian holds my gaze, and the pity within them makes my stomach churn. "The racai got to Valindor before I could. I could not leave you, Thalia."

"*Leave me?*" I sputter. "*Leave. Me?*"

I laugh, yet it is crazed, bordering on the verge of hysterical.

"You did not think for *one-second* Valindor was of more importance?"

He stiffens.

"Elders, Killian! After all we went through to retrieve that sword, how could you have been so foolish?"

His jaw sets. "I was not *foolish—*"

I throw my hands up, weaving my fingers together and clasping them with crushing force. "You let them take Valindor, Killian. Did you even *try* to save it?"

"Of course, I tried," he snaps. "It was you or Valindor, Thalia. I was not going to let you *die*."

I sink my hands into my hair, rumpling the already tangled strands as I tremble with rage. Furious tears prickle my eyes.

"Maybe you should have—"

"Thalia!" He bellows.

I fall silent, meeting his gaze with fierce, watery eyes.

His features are drawn, and his jaw is clenched. He holds my gaze with a stern one of his own, eyes clouded and flashing with rage, yet I do not miss the undertone of grief.

"There is nothing for me to say, Killian."

The tension leaves his body, and I notice the subtle sag in his usually bold shoulders.

I walk away, head pounding.

"Thalia." I hear Alistar clamber to his feet, grunting against the pain. "Thalia, wait—"

"*No*," I whirl towards the rest of my company, hair whipping with the movement. "I do not want to hear your words of reassurance; your sympathy means nothing to me. I did not come this far just to watch Valindor slip away. Never in my life have I met such *cowards*."

With nothing else to say, I tread into the bushes.

Nobody follows me.

\*

Not far from our makeshift camp, there is a small creek. The water is crystal clear, gushing in smooth waves over the pebbles that line the bottom. They are piled upon one another, greys, browns, blacks, and light blues. Together, they create a mesmerising effect, the water rippling about them like the sun on a hot day. I stare at the pebbles, observing them. The difference in their shapes and sizes. Their various colours. The way the water moves around them, parting where they breach the surface.

I lean forward, plucking one from the base of the stream. Holding it before me, I watch the rain hit its face, trailing down its surface. I follow the droplet as it plummets to the ground.

"Thalia?"

Abash, I drop the rock, pushing away from the stream and standing abruptly, bringing another wave of minor nausea. I steady myself before looking to Killian from the corner of my eye.

He says nothing more, instead watching the breeze rustle the leaves on the opposite side of the brook. His hands are clasped behind his back, and he moves his thumb idly back and forth against his knuckles. I refocus on the creek, wincing against the heaviness of my skull.

A fragile silence echoes between us.

After a while, Killian clears his throat. His lips part in an attempt to speak, yet I do not give him the chance.

"Save your breath, Killian. I am not interested in what you have to say."

He blinks, once, unexpectedly calm.

"Let me speak."

I turn towards him, anger sizzling in the pit of my stomach. "Your words mean nothing to me, Killian. You cannot change what you have done."

He pivots abruptly, stepping up to me, tilting his head down to better meet my gaze. He is taller than I — intimidatingly tall — and stands a few inches above me, and with his broad, muscular build and piercing silver eyes, he is easily able to unnerve his rival.

Yet I know him too well to allow his infuriation to deter me.

"You cannot expect me to have left you, Thalia. That beast could have cracked your *skull*, and I would not, *could* not leave you for dead. Elders, how you are still alive, I do not know," his words are brittle.

"If leaving me meant the racai would not have claimed Valindor, I would have *wanted* you to abandon me. You know that," I snarl.

"You would have *died*."

"Then so be it!"

"You would sacrifice yourself for a *blade?*"

"If that is the price that must be paid to keep Valindor from falling into the hands of Sindir, then I am prepared to pay it!"

"Well, I am not," he hollers.

I step up to him so that we are a mere hair's breadth apart and tilt my chin to meet his stern gaze. "Some sacrifices must be made."

I step away from him, yet he catches my wrists, pulling me roughly against him. When he looks down at me, the hard edge of his gaze is gone, replaced by a new kind of tenderness. "Not you, Thalia. *You* are not a sacrifice I am willing to make."

I tense, caught off guard by his words. His gaze continues to hold

21

mine, and striking, crystal blue eyes flit over my face, then search my own emerald ones. Our bodies are flush as he holds me against him, awaiting a reply, and I feel my lips part, yet remain unaware of how to respond. With his body pressed against mine, I can feel the rapid beat of his heart against my chest, see the flex of his throat when he swallows, eyes continuing their warm search of my own.

The nervousness radiating from his body jerks me back into reality. The *fear*.

I take a shuddering breath, scanning his face momentarily before bringing my eyes back to his. I swallow the lump of emotion clawing up my throat and replace it with the relentless fury that churns in my stomach.

I do not forgive him for what he has done, no matter how good his intentions.

Leaning forward until our faces are mere inches apart, I allow the burning rage to seep into my words, quiet and harsh. "Then you are *selfish*."

I break away, disentangling myself from his arms and am shocked to see the hurt on his face. He quickly regains himself, concealing his pain with raw fury. His face flushes with anger, and a vein pulses in his neck.

I tilt my chin up in response, then start down the stream, away from Killian.

"Elders—" he hisses. "You do not get it, do you?"

I swivel around, equally as furious. "Understand *what*, Killian? What is there for me to understand?" I step forward once again, a vicious pounding in my ears. "You let those beasts get away with Valindor. We worked tirelessly for that relic, and you let it get swept in your effort to save me. Did you consider the consequences? If Sindir gets his hands on Valindor, we are doomed. Everybody in these lands is *doomed*, Killian, and thousands of lives will be lost. I watched Calivar's kingdom and everybody within it *burn*. I lost my father because of this blade. I gave up my life in Lsthrain, and it was *not* for this. So tell me, Killian, what do you want me to understand?"

Killian throws his head back to the sky, running a rough hand through his hair. He squeezes his eyes shut, fist clenched.

"Oh, Thalia," he breathes, deflated.

I lift my chin fiercely, tears building behind my eyes, burning with rage and emotion. "I did not think you could be such a fool, throwing away the fate of these lands to save one life. To save *me*. I am not worth that sacrifice, Killian."

His chest hitches, and he stares at me, unmoving.

"You are right, Thalia," he says, his voice low, rough. His throat bobs as he swallows, and he meets my gaze, staring intently into my eyes for a moment. The sorrow behind them breaks my heart.

"I suppose love makes fools of us all."

With that, he turns, vanishing into the wood.

# THREE
## THALIA

I stand frozen, staring at the spot where Killian had stood, breath caught in my throat.

*Love makes fools of us all.*

His words replay in my mind, an endless track of the same six words. Over and over they play, a never-ending track of sorrow and regret. It cuts through my body, shredding me apart until I am breathless and trembling with emotion. It rips me apart from the inside, its sharp claws sinking into my heart and tearing it apart until it is nothing but meaningless pieces. My chest is heavy with unshed tears, and I dig my teeth into my lip, wrapping my arms around myself as I sink to the rocky shore.

Grief chokes me in its icy vice, throttling me against all my foolishness. Tears burn across my cheeks, each one carving a new path across my skin. They leave a trail of fire in their wake, flames crackling with the pressure of my despair.

*Love makes fools of us all.*

Every time the words replay, I feel my heart twist painfully. Feel my heart twist over and over again until it feels as though it may burst. His words have a thousand meanings, ones I am afraid to decipher, so I do not allow myself to open such a door, to dig so deep into his phrase for fear I shall uncover something best kept hidden.

I do not let myself dwell on it.

*Cannot.*

Because this heaviness in my heart, this sickness, it is a disease, spreading through my veins and making my stomach lurch and flutter, spreading to claw at my ribs and climb my throat. It is everything fighting to be set free, to be said and expressed.

Everything I cannot.

Everything I dare not, for fear of what such things may be, for fear of the truths they may reveal.

So instead, I squeeze my eyes shut, blocking the world out, for it is too much.

I have lost too much.

My place in Lsthrain.

Calivar.

Enia.

And now Killian.

And if I do not have Killian, then who do I have?

The accomplices I have known for mere days?

They do not know me as he does, do not understand me as he does. He and I share a bond different from any other, one I thought unbreakable.

And how wrong I was, for now, I have lost him, the only person I truly have left.

We have lost each other to our own selfishness.

All for a simple blade.

A blade that is now in the possession of our enemy, the lone person we vowed it would not fall to.

Killian and I have fought before, but never like this. This time, I have gone too far, pushed over the edge by my grief, fear and anger. The emotions I failed to express. The emotions I was too *afraid* to express for fear that I would be perceived as weak.

It seems that was a mistake.

Killian's words reverberate through my skull, and I press my hands to either side of my head to relinquish the pounding. My eyes fall closed, and I erase his words from my mind, no longer able to listen to their rhythm of heartache.

Remembering the anguish in his eyes when he spoke them shatters my heart anew.

I wrap my arms around my knees, burying my face. Tears stain the fabric of my pants, as cold and unforgiving as the rain, and I let the sorrow envelope me, suffocating me in its inescapable grasp. I let the sobs wrack my body until I am trembling, until the rain has seeped into my skin, and I am shivering, my skull hammering with the weight of my pain and recent injury.

The hope that once thrived is now gone, diminished with the theft of Valindor. The racai have it in their possession. Once they reach Orathin, it will be passed to Sindir. He will destroy Valindor and resume rule, bringing every kingdom to its knees in search of the power to rule these lands once more. And although he does not yet have such power, with Valindor destroyed, nothing can stop him from gaining it.

The land will be cast into an eternal war.

I choke on a sob, pressing my hands against my eyes to suppress a new stream of tears. My chest heaves with a ragged breath, and I raise my head. Sniffing, I press the back of my hand against my lips to muffle my cries.

Desperate to focus on something other than my sorrow, I shift my attention to the other side of the stream, studying the wood. The trees sway gently, their leaves dipping and curving in a perfectly choreographed dance. Rain pours down their faces, leaving a damp trail in their wake. The drops fall to the ground, absorbed by the rough soil. My eyes scan the trunks. Rough and sturdy, streaked with grooves and small crevices. The rain trails through the canals, creating a map of tiny rivers. The trees remain tall, sprouting fresh leaves each year. So many storms they have lived through, so many years where the winter has been relentless with cold, hopeless in the search for spring.

And yet they live on.

Blemished they may be, but they remain tall, unwavering against the batter of rain and bitter chill.

I wipe away my tears, blinking to clear my vision.

Too many have died over Valindor. Too many have died for me to give up, to sit and weep in a pool of my own pitiful tears.

We still have time. The racai will not have yet reached Orathin. We can retrieve it and then journey back to Endalin to plan our next move.

These lands are not yet lost.

I push myself onto my feet, brushing away the mud and grime. Releasing a shuddering breath, I clear my mind. I cannot allow myself to dwell on what I have lost.

*It is ill-advised to dwell on the past if you wish to change the future.*

Killian's words echo in my mind, and my heart throbs painfully. Despite my anger, my grief, I will not allow myself to sit idly whilst the fate of these lands is at risk.

With newfound determination, I turn towards our camp and make haste for my accomplices.

# FOUR
## THALIA

he camp is silent as I break free of the trees, stepping into the view of my allies.

All heads swivel in my direction, and I am suddenly painfully aware of how flushed I shall be from crying, how puffy and bloodshot my eyes shall be. I tilt my chin up to allow for a display of confidence, for wiping my eyes shall only add to their suspicion. Alistar, Thorne, and Aliya remain in camp, yet Killian is not to be seen. I take a calming breath, not allowing myself to appear daunted.

Not a word is spoken.

"Well?" I ask, letting my gaze drift between the three of them, who remain staring. I raise my eyebrows. "Do you have nothing better to do than sit and gawk at me?"

Aliya quickly averts her gaze, refocusing her attention on Alistar's injury, which she continues to tend to with a makeshift bandage. Alistar clears his throat, looking awkwardly back to Aliya and watching as she wraps his wound.

It is clear my argument with Killian was overheard, for their uncomfortable expressions and the little space between the camp and

29

stream are a giveaway.

The tension in the air is thick, weighing down upon us and caging us in with invisible walls.

I spot Alwyne tied to an oak tree and make my way to his side. He whinnies with excitement, dragging his hoof through the damp grass. I lift my hands to cup his nose, letting my fingers brush over his thick coat. He snorts in response, closing his eyes against my touch. I rest my head against his, comforted slightly by the sense of calm that washes over me. After a moment, he nudges me gently, sensing my distress.

When I finally raise my head, I let my hands drop, running a hand beneath his mane as I move to my satchel. Flipping it open, I search for my waterskin. The pounding in my head has resumed, more jarring than before. Pulling it free, I take a swig of the cool water. Nausea boils in the pit of my stomach, but I have not the heart to address it.

"What food do we have remaining?" I ask.

Thorne looks up from where he sits at the fire. The dead rabbit dangles above the flames, roasting. He leans back, crossing his arms over his chest.

"None. Save for this." He jerks his head, gesturing towards the animal. "Although if you had not thrown the last of Killian's berries away in your haste, we would have more."

I slam my satchel shut.

"Do not—"

"*Enough.*"

Killian's voice echoes through the wood, harsh and biting. He steps into view, carrying small pouches that are brimming with berries. Deep red juice stains their fabric. Moving toward our accomplices, he tosses them each a pouch. But when he reaches me, he throws it without a word, refusing to meet my eyes or glance in my direction. He maintains his distance.

And I let him.

I do not thank him as I open the bag, my stomach grumbling at the sight of the fresh berries. I pop a few into my mouth, and sweet, earthy flavour dances over my tongue.

"How long was I unconscious?" I ask.

There is a beat of silence.

"A day," Alistar replies.

I scold myself for the time I have wasted but press on.

"The racai are only a day ahead of us, then."

A hush falls over the camp, and four pairs of eyes turn in my direction, wide with surprise. Alistar's features draw with confusion.

"Pardon me?"

"The racai," I say. "They must only be a day ahead of us. We can reclaim Valindor. We have not yet lost."

Killian scoffs.

Slowly, I pivot to face him, an edge to my gaze. He stands at Elwis's side, adjusting his tack. His back is to me.

"Do you care to add to the conversation, Killian?" Poison laces my words.

He turns to me, leaning back against Elwis. He crosses his arms over

31

his broad chest, quirking an eyebrow.

"You wish to pursue the racai?" He asks, mocking.

"Yes. Will that be an issue?"

His eyes narrow to slits.

"After all of *that,* Thalia? After our argument? You walk away as if nothing happened, claiming you wish to *pursue* the racai?"

"You expect me to just *quit?*" I snap.

"No, I do not. There has never been a time you have, yet I question the time it took you to come to this realisation. I question the way you spoke to me, angered that I sacrificed Valindor for *you,* Thalia. And now you simply wish to pursue it, as if it is only now an option? Only an option to reclaim it *after* what you said to me?" He spits. "You should have realised this before, Thalia. You should have been grateful that I saved you, should have looked past our loss and decided to track down the racai the moment you learned of them possessing it."

I tilt my head, disbelief drawing my brows together. "Forgive me, Killian." My words lack conviction and are instead laced with sarcasm. "I *am* grateful, but it does not make you any less selfish. You knew you should have saved Valindor, you knew what was at stake, and you still chose to save me. Now they are a day ahead of us, growing closer to Orathin as we speak. If Valindor is delivered to Sindir before we can get to them, we have already lost. *Every. Single. Kingdom. Every. Single. Life* in Ilya is at stake. *Yes,* we still have a chance, but we could have had the advantage, Killian. We could have had Sindir at *our* mercy. We could have had the upper hand. But you gave it all away for *me.*"

A low growl rises in his throat, and he pushes himself away from Elwis, his eyes flashing. "A *chance*, Thalia. That is all we need. That is all we had when we began this journey. You think any of this could have been accomplished without you?" He waves at our makeshift camp, at our accomplices, who listen to every word we speak. "No, it could not. And it cannot be finished without you."

He stops a few feet short of me, and for a moment, he just stares, his cold eyes locked on mine.

"Does it make me a villain, Thalia, for sacrificing these lands to save you?"

I tilt my chin up, swallowing thickly. "Maybe."

He nods, clucking his tongue. "Well, I would rather be the villain that works by your side than the hero you oppose."

His words shoot straight to my heart, and I take a step away from him, shaking my head to try and clear my jumbled thoughts. "No. No. You did not *work* by my side during that battle, did you? You may have saved me, but you sacrificed everything we have worked for. I may have started this, Killian, but tell me, what makes *me* so special?"

He is silent.

After a moment, he says, "Fine, Thalia," voice low, dangerous. "Pursue them if that is what you wish; it is clear I hold no sway over you."

He returns to Elwis's side, and I step towards him, seething.

"That is it?"

He halts, body growing rigid.

"What more do you want, Thalia?"

My lips part, and I shake my head, disbelieving. "I—"

A realisation dawns upon me, and I feel my eyebrows knit together.

"You speak as if you shall not follow me in this pursuit."

"I will not."

"*Pardon?*" I sputter.

"I will not be accompanying you in your pursuit."

My jaw grows slack as I search for something to say, yet I am incapable of finding any that shall suffice. I can do nothing but stare at him, lips parted in silence.

"How can you simply 'not accompany us'?"

He turns to face me. His expression is dark, his features drawn, and his jaw clenched.

"Now that the racai have Valindor, they will be rallying their forces against Lsthrain. They have an alliance with the trolls, if you recall. I shall return there, where I will fight alongside my kingdom."

Anger swells in the pit of my stomach.

"You would leave us?" I ask. "You would leave us when everything is falling apart, when *we* are falling apart? You would leave at the first opportunity when the consequences of sacrificing Valindor are thrust upon you?"

He whirls towards me, eyes flashing with rage.

"Lsthrain is my *home*," he snarls.

"As it is mine."

And then Killian is marching towards me, the fury in his expression unlike anything he has shown me before. This is harsh, unyielding rage. I back away from him, yet he follows until I am forced against a tree, the rough trunk biting into my back. He places a hand on the coarse bark above my head and towers over me. He leans forward, his face mere inches from my own. The impending danger I sense in his voice imposes upon me the sentience of his rage.

There is no mistaking it, the silent fury hidden beneath the walls he has built, the calm he uses as a guise.

A tendril of fear encases my heart.

His words are like ice against my cheek. "Lsthrain is not your home. You made that clear the moment you left."

And they cut me like a knife.

I recoil, my lips parting to form a response, yet all I can do is stutter.

"I—"

That is it. I feel my heart shatter into a thousand minuscule pieces, pieces too small to ever be put together again. I have endured many hardships in my life, but Killian's words are a different kind of pain, a different kind of tear in my soul.

*Especially* when they come from someone I care for so dearly.

Tears sting my eyes, but I wipe them away furiously. Swallowing my agony, I place my hands against his strong chest, shoving him away from me.

"Do what you please, Killian."

I duck beneath his arm, stepping around him and putting as much distance between us as possible.

I do not acknowledge the sympathetic glances of the others.

Nor do I say a word as Killian prepares to ride.

Nor when he mounts Elwis, then vanishes into the forest.

# FIVE
## THALIA

The next while is spent in silence.

Thorne sits by the fire, poking the wood with a charred stick. He works to rearrange the logs; the flames reflected in his dark eyes as the last dregs of daylight begin to fade. Both Aliya and Alistar have joined him about the fire. The two sit together on a downed log, chatting quietly. Occasionally, somebody glances my way, yet they quickly avert their gaze when I meet their pitiful expressions.

Alistar, despite his weakness and injury, remains the spirited man I had first met. He tries to lighten the mood, to no avail.

Absently, my fingers trace the cold gold hilt of my dagger whilst I stare blankly ahead, the thick trunks and swirl of leaves a blur before me. My mind is restless, weaving through a fog of jumbled, unfinished thoughts and bitter emotions to conjure a plan.

The racai will be on their way to Orathin, yet the kingdom's location is one I do not know. I cannot find them if I do not know their heading.

"Where is the nearest village?" I ask.

Their hushed conversation ceases. Thorne's eyebrows knit together as he shares a wary glance with Alistar and Aliya.

"Not far, depending on the route you take. A day at the most. If you continue south, you shall find Verila," Thorne says.

Standing, I nod. "Good. Assuming none of you knows the location of Orathin, we shall venture to Verila, so we may find a map to guide us to Sindir's kingdom."

Silence.

I raise my eyebrows, daring them to question me.

Alistar opens his mouth, then closes it. His lips curve into a frown, and he tries to stand. Aliya ducks beneath his arm, helping him up.

"Thalia, I—" he hesitates.

"Speak, Alistar; I have dealt with enough today and can be hurt no further. So please, save me the time and speak your mind."

"I do not think it wise, Thalia," Aliya cuts in, prompting him. "Not to leave so soon. Both you and Alistar are badly injured; you need time to rest, time to heal." She motions to Alistar's wound. "Dare I say it shall be hard for Alistar to travel with such an injury, especially when we inevitably cross paths with our enemy."

I say nothing, allowing my gaze to shift between my allies. They stare at me in return, awaiting my response. Conflicted, I offer them a reluctant nod. I cannot deny the truth in Aliya's words. Alistar is a liability and shall endanger us further should we encounter our enemy.

"Thorne?" I ask, setting my gaze on him.

He surveys a point beyond me, contemplating. When he finally brings his gaze to mine, a shadow of regret flits across his expression.

"My duty is to Aliya."

I deflate at his words, yet cannot let it deter me. "Then I travel alone."

"Thalia—" Alistar starts toward me, his features curved into a grimace as he staggers, eyes wide with alarm. Yet his wound prevents him from moving without assistance, and he trips. Aliya quickly steadies him, but it is not without a struggle, for he is far bigger and heavier than her.

He is in no condition to continue.

My heart twinges in response, saddened by having to continue without them.

Although I have not known these people for long, I have grown fond of them.

"You cannot do such a thing, Thalia," he states.

"I can do as I please."

"It is too dangerous. The racai likely remain within these woods, and you are wounded. You are lucky to be alive after our last battle, do not push yourself."

"I know my limits," I fire back.

"And yet you cease to abide by them."

I pivot to face him. "Do not pretend to know me, Alistar. I am far more complex than you believe."

His soft features curve into a glare, and he clenches his jaw.

"You cannot deny my words," he admonishes.

"No, I cannot. Yet I have made my decision, and nothing you say is capable of changing that."

Without another word, I drop down against the tall oak where I had first awoken. My cloak remains in the damp soil, and I pick it up, shaking the dirt off before swinging it around my neck and clipping it. Sinking back against the trunk, I pull its edges tight against me, finding little comfort in its warmth.

Despite my resolution to not succumb to not heartache, I cannot ignore Killian's absence. Nor the acute sense of emptiness that clutches my heart.

# SIX
## KILLIAN

The rain falls steadier now.

It pours without relent, battering the leaves above me into surrender. Yet their canopy is unaffected, creating a shield against the unyielding chill. Still, many drops breach their barricade, seeping into my skin and soaking my hair. A shiver rakes my body, and I tighten my fingers about the reins, a defence against the layer of ice encasing my heart.

Yet the bitter cold is not what pains me most.

Thalia's words ricochet in my head, rattling my skull until I can no longer stand the agony.

Never before have we fought so tirelessly, so ruthlessly.

It was not my intent to lose Valindor, yet I could not save the sword and Thalia both. For Thalia, it was life or death.

And I was not going to let her die.

No matter the cost.

I release a breath, trying to ease the pain in my heart, which throbs painfully.

It hurt me to leave her.

Somewhere in my cold heart, I know it was my fault for allowing the racai to regain Valindor, yet her reaction infuriates me.

I did what I had to in order to keep her alive.

I did it for *her*.

But also for myself because I refuse to live in a world without Thalia.

*Then you are selfish.*

She could not have expected me to leave her. Not after everything we have been through together. Not after all our years of unyielding friendship. It is not fair. And neither was her reaction.

I allowed the racai to gain Valindor so she could live. She should have been grateful. Instead, she was enraged.

A heady price I paid, a price Thalia was not willing to pay. Not even for her life.

But it was a price *I* was willing to pay, and I would not change my decision, even if I possessed such power.

*Sacrifices must be made*, she had said.

Our friendship may be that price.

My anger has overcome me, for I could not persuade myself to accompany her in her pursuit. Not when her words cut so deep, not when the wound is so fresh. A rash decision, one I know I shall regret.

Thalia does not forgive easily.

Stubborn girl. Clenching my jaw, I fight the anger boiling in my stomach. Her rage antagonises me, and the memory of the raw, undilated anger in her eyes only heightens my fury.

I kick Elwis's sides, and she hastens her pace.

I am eager to put as much space between myself and this wretched place as I can, no matter how much it hurts.

No matter the way my heart beats in agony as I travel further from our accomplices.

From Thalia.

# SEVEN
## THALIA

I am awake before the others.

It is long before dawn when I rise, stirred by the anxiety that consumes my mind. Stiff, I let the hood of my cloak fall away, and I stretch my arms, grasping my hands above my head to regain some feeling in them. When the tension in my body eases, I slump back against the tree, my eyes fluttering closed once more.

My night has been restless, my sleep scarce, broken by the rush of my thoughts, the tingle in my stomach, and the pain in my skull.

The sun has not yet breached the horizon, and the forest remains in a blanket of semi-darkness. Although I try to fall back to sleep, I cannot. My mind is too restless, too on edge, and my emotions still too fresh. Instead, I pull myself onto my feet, huddling into my cloak as the chill pierces my skin.

The air is damp, thick with the remnants of yesterday's rainfall. Yet the sky no longer weeps; instead, it has wiped away its tears, clearing the rain away. Nevertheless, its sorrow remains, its once warm blue surrendered by the heavy grey clouds.

Careful with my footing, I tread silently to Alwyne's side. He remains asleep, and I bring my hand to the bridge of his nose, brushing his soft coat gently.

His eyes waft open.

Groggy and unfocused, he relaxes into my touch, eyes fluttering open, then closed. He snorts quietly.

A smile tugs at my lips, yet it feels forced. I drop his head, moving to his side as I check the contents of my satchel.

I have few supplies remaining. Nothing but my almost empty waterskin and pouch of berries remain. I am painfully aware of my hunger, but cannot afford to waste what few nutrients I have left in case something should go wrong. The village is a day's ride from here, at most. My supplies shall last until then, and I shall replenish them when I arrive.

I proceed to check, then adjust my tack. I plan to reach Verila as soon as I can, for no more time can be wasted, I must pursue the racai.

I must reach them before they arrive at Orathin.

When I am happy with the assuredness of my tack, I wake Alwyne. Although drowsy, he makes no protest when I urge him to prepare for our journey.

Once his bonds are broken, I lead him away from the tree, gripping the pommel of my saddle.

"You are leaving so soon?"

I drop my hand, turning to face Alistar. He remains by the fire, his back pressed against the fallen log. Aliya sleeps soundly beside him, her head upon his shoulder, cloak wrapped tightly about her.

45

"I have already wasted too much time."

Alistar sighs, and his eyes drift to the surrounding forest, a certain sad calmness coming about them. "None of this is your fault. It is not your duty to pursue Valindor. You do not have to do this alone, Thalia."

I lean back against Alwyne, jaw tightening against a rush of emotion. "Yes, I do. Killian is gone,"— my voice cracks — "And you are too weak to continue with me. I should never have brought you into this, any of you. I started this, and I shall end it, whether or not I am alone in my quest."

He stares at me then, his eyebrows drawing together—a troubled frown tugs at his lips.

"I cannot stop you, then?"

"No, you cannot."

He nods, reluctant in his acceptance. "If I cannot accompany you, then at least let me assist you." He reaches into his pocket and pulls out a few gold coins. He flips them to me.

"You will need currency for your travels. Staying in a village such as Verila cannot be done for free. You will need to pay for a place to stay and a map."

I look down at the coins, brushing my thumb over their cold surface. It is engraved with a horse's head. These are not easy to come by.

"I cannot accept these." I hold them out to him.

"What use are they to me out here? You need them more than I."

"You will need them when you return to Endalin."

He shakes his head. "What I have is enough to survive on, and that is all I need."

I close my fist over the coins, then slip them into my satchel. "Thank you."

He bows his head. "Be careful, Thalia."

Hoisting myself onto Alwyne's back, I take a hold of the reins, then drop my head, returning the gesture.

"I shall. Take care of yourself and the others."

He dips his head. "Of course."

With nothing else to say, I depart into the forest.

# EIGHT
## THALIA

travel at a steady pace, keeping distance from the treacherous paths and exposed clearings. The forest is quiet, its unsettling silence broken only by the gentle chirp of birds or the rustle of leaves. Occasionally, a rodent will scurry past, catching Alwyne off guard.

I remain wary throughout the entirety of my journey, the slightest disturbance forcing my hand to fall upon my dagger.

When the sun has breached the canopy of leaves, I decide to stop at a nearby stream. The golden rays illuminate the particles of dust and brighten the forest's greenery.

The brook shimmers, clear water sparkling with morning light. I drop down from Alwyne's back, swinging the reins over his head. He whinnies in response, following me to the water.

I run my hand beneath his mane as he dips his head, drinking from the glistening creek. Patting his coat, I lower myself onto my knees, leaning over the brook.

My reflection gazes back at me.

Red-rimmed eyes and blood-spotted cheeks, skin caked in dirt and scratches, and tangled, mud-crusted hair.

*I catch a glimpse of my reflection. Long hair cast over my shoulders, draping down my back. My vibrant emerald eyes shine against the bright, cloudless sky beyond me.*

*Movement catches my eye, and then another figure rippling in the reflection: light, golden blonde hair, pale blue eyes, and broad shoulders.*

My heart throbs at the memory, the memory of a better time, of a time when I was not alone, of a time I was not so desperate or hopeless or worn.

Of a time when Killian was by my side.

I drop my head into my hands, releasing a breath. I am a mess. My emotions are a mess. This situation is a mess. *Everything* is a mess.

Killian and I are a mess.

I lift my head, sliding back to stretch my legs before me. My hands fidget in my lap as I try to make sense of everything.

So many thoughts. So many emotions. They jumble in my mind, making it hard to think straight.

What chaos I have created.

Sighing, I edge closer to the stream, pulling off my leather boots. Rolling up my pants, I bring myself to stand. I wade into the cool water, finding a rock in the centre of the creek. Sitting upon it, I cup my hands and dunk them below the surface. The water weaves between my fingers, creating a mesmerising ripple. I splash the water over my face, washing away the blood and grime. Beneath the layer of dirt is a single scratch on my cheek, represented by a faint red line. I brush my fingers over it. There is no pain.

That is when I notice the blood beneath my nails. I dip them into the water again, scrubbing it away. When they are clean, I pour water over my hair, rinsing it free of filth.

Once done, I look back at my reflection. Free of blood and dirt, my face has returned to normal. Smooth skin, soft red lips, emerald eyes, long lashes. My lips tug into a frown.

I run my fingers through my damp hair, working to free the knots. When I am finished, I stand upon the rock, taking in my surroundings. The wood is cast in a golden glow, vibrant green leaves swaying in the soft breeze. Birds call to one another from their perch, occasionally drifting over the brook to meet one another.

If I were not so dispirited, I may have smiled.

Instead, I tread back to shore, unrolling my pants and tugging my boots on. I pull my hair over my shoulder, blowing a stubborn strand out of my eye.

Alwyne digs his hoof into the ground, throwing his head back to the sky and shaking his mane. He snorts quietly, a sadness behind his eyes.

"Alwyne," I whisper, stepping up before him. He nuzzles me, resting his head against my stomach. I can sense the unease rolling off of him. Gently, I run my hand over his coat, a silent reassurance.

"Come on," I say, taking his head in my hands. "We shall be all right." My voice is low, and I struggle to convince myself that my words are true.

"You will eat properly when we reach the village. You can rest there."

He lifts his head, eyes sparkling.

"We must go."

I grasp the pommel, swinging my leg over and settling into the saddle. I pat his neck once before taking the reins.

I do not know what will await us in Verila, but I cling to these last shards of hope.

With nothing more than that, we continue toward the village.

# NINE
## KILLIAN

rode through the night.

It was cold and damp, the darkness echoing with the sound of past battles.

Recent battles.

Our battles.

It is not hard to recall the clash of blades, nor the guttural cries of each beast as they were slain. Distinctly, I remember the way their dark blood splattered my face, staining the ground around me as they fell to their knees. I remember watching the light blink out of their piercing eyes.

A shiver clambers up my spine, and I tremble. Gripping the reins tighter, I ball my hands into fists to stop my shaking.

*Weak.*

*So weak.*

My emotions have bested me, and I drown in a pit of my own sorrow and anger. Regret. No matter how hard I try to suppress them, to feel nothing but ire. To convince myself that leaving Thalia and our accomplices was the right decision. That I am doing the right thing by returning to Lsthrain, my kingdom, and fighting alongside my people.

I fail to do so every time.

I let my anger for Thalia win me over.

And what a fool it has made me.

Yet I know I cannot turn back now. I refuse to.

She despises me.

And a part of me understands why. The other hates her back.

And yet, I ask myself, is it truly hate?

Yes.

*Yes,* I convince myself, *it is.*

But deep down, I know I lie to myself.

Elwis breaks through the trees, and we emerge into a clearing. Endalin glitters in the early morning light, not far in the distance. I press my leg into Elwis's side, directing her towards the pond, which lies adjacent to the kingdom. She moves back into the tree line, just out of view of the sentries, who patrol the surrounding wall.

I do not wish for another encounter with Faodén, especially without the presence of his men and daughter. He will question their absence, as well as our knowledge of Valindor.

If we retrieved it.

I do not have the will to explain to him the truth.

So I stick within the tree line of the forest, for if the guards recognise me, I shall lose all chance of avoiding the king.

Continuing within the wood, we circle the pond, heading towards the valley. I study the small body of water. The water shimmers with early morning rays, granting it a sparkling effect. Occasionally, the water ripples and a fish breaches the surface, leaping into the air before diving back down with a splash. Beyond, the branches sway gently, leaves rustling against one another. The weaker trunks bend with the gentle breeze.

Elwis whinnies, rearing her head.

I reach down to pat her neck, and she snorts in response.

She shakes her head in the direction of the pond, and I drop my hand away from her coat.

"We cannot stop here. You may drink when we reach the valley."

She paws the ground impatiently, then flicks her tail. Nevertheless, she continues around the pool.

When we reach the far side, the sunlight is cast upon us. The golden banners radiate with heat, warming my body. My eyes begin to droop, the sudden warmth giving way to my exhaustion.

I have not slept for over a day, and my energy has begun to wane. My eyes fall closed, and I sway.

Elwis stumbles, and I jerk awake.

I clench my jaw, exhaustion only heightening my anger. Aggravated, I click my tongue, motioning for Elwis to hasten her pace. She does as I command, moving into a trot.

We travel around the pond, breaking free of the tree line just beyond Endalin. Elwis transitions into a canter, moving swiftly through the tall-grass field. The blades ripple about us, parting to make way. The stems brush my legs, and I drop one hand from the reins, letting it fall into the sea of grass. They weave between my fingers, tickling the palm of my hand.

When we reach the edge of the field, we slow to a walk. The grass fades to pebbles, and the river appears before me. Glistening and calm, it is a mirrored reflection of the pond, with brilliant blue waters that sparkle beneath the sun.

Once out of Endalin's view, I direct Elwis to the shoreline. We stop for only as long as we need. Elwis is able to quench her thirst whilst I clean the blood and grim from my face and hair. I scan the forest behind me, gaze settling on a nestle of trees.

Standing, I run a hand through my hair, damp from the rinse I have given it. I whistle to Elwis, who quickly returns to my side. When I pat her coat, a tuft of hair wafts into the air.

I take her reins, pulling them over her head. Leading her towards the forest, I tread carefully through the thick undergrowth and twisted roots. When I reach the crowd of trees, I swing the reins over Elwis's head, running my hand over the bridge of her nose. She snorts gently, dropping her head to the ground.

"We will continue soon, rest while you can," I tell her, expecting no response.

Dropping down before a thick-trunked tree, I tilt my head back to stare at the leaves. The branches are so crammed with leaves that the sunlight is unable to break through, offering me a reprieve from the growing heat. The forest here is dense. Denser than the Forest of Undying Souls. Denser than the forest leading to the Burial Grounds.

On horseback, it would be impossible to navigate. The thick roots and heavy underbrush crowd the space between trees, which clump together in an impenetrable mass.

My hand falls to the hilt of my dagger, seeking its reassurance. Without Thalia or my accomplices, there is nobody to take the watch whilst I sleep. I must rely on my survival skills and remain wary. The hilt of my dagger is cool, the gold smooth beneath my touch. I let my head rest against the tree, and it does not take long for my eyes to flutter closed.

I drift into a deep, unbroken sleep.

# TEN
## THALIA

We arrive by nightfall.

Verila is a small, crime-ridden village, set just beyond the trees of this wretched forest.

Having navigated onto a broad path, Alwyne now moves at a slow walk. The surrounding forest is wider spread and more open than it is deeper into this wood, allowing me a better view and awareness of my surroundings.

Exhaustion has finally taken its pure, relentless hold upon Alwyne. His head is lowered, eyes often fluttering closed, then snapping open. Occasionally, I must squeeze my legs against his sides to awaken him. I, too, am worn out, for I did not sleep well last night and am tired from a day of travelling.

When we breach the border of trees, the city is set at the end of a rugged pebble pathway encased by a low stone wall. Yet it can be nothing more than a mere architectural quality, as it poses no threat, no intimidation. No assurance in keeping its residents safe. Crumbling and rotten at the edges, the stones begin to fall away from each other, the cracks between largening, spurting greenery.

Alwyne halts at the end of the trail. I look up, surveying the top of the wall. There is a single flag, tattered and caked in mud; it does poorly in representing its village.

No sentries patrol it.

"State your business." A man's voice catches my attention. Slowly, I bring my gaze down to him.

A short, gruff old man. He sits in a rickety chair beside the gate. A white stubble runs the length of his chin. It is spotted with dirt, as is his hair, which is cloaked by a black hood. Eyes, so dark they appear black, search me, running every inch of Alwyne and me. They settle momentarily on my satchels before returning to my face. He narrows his eyes.

"I seek shelter for the night," I say, an edge of authority to my voice.

His eyebrows draw together, and he stands unsteadily. He wears pants that are too long for him and worn boots. A cane rests in his hand, digging into the dirt beside him to support his slanted stature.

"What be yer reasons for staying here, then? Got yourself into some trouble, eh?" His voice is laced with suspicion.

"Call it trouble if you will," I reply.

"I see." He steps forward, arm quivering as he presses his weight onto the cane. "Shall it provide a problem for my village? Ain't being chased, are ya?"

My eyes narrow, growing impatient with the man's scepticism. I need no more problems, especially not an old man who poses to protect his village when I am sure he would crumble without the support of his stick.

"My trouble is my own. I pose no threat to you nor your village, besides." I motion to the decaying wall, remaining carefully composed. "It would seem you need the business."

His lip pulls back, revealing chipped and stained teeth. He bares them at me, a low snarl erupting from his throat. I do nothing in return, determined to save him the satisfaction.

Despite his reluctance, he hobbles away from me, opening the gates. I nod to him as I pass through, yet refrain from meeting his withering gaze.

The village is dimly lit. Few torches are alight, resting warily within their sconces. A strong wind whips their flames into a spiral, a tornado of fire illuminating the structures in an eerie light. The buildings are made of wood, most at a precarious slant. They tilt forward into the street, looming over me, threatening. Through their cracked and grimy windows, shadows dance across the walls, their figures scarcely illuminated in firelight. Many of the buildings are bars, full to the brim of drunk men and women. Others are darkened stores, empty until morning.

As I continue through the cobblestone streets, the noise only heightens. Shouts rise from inside the bars, often followed by the crash of a table being overturned or a glass being shattered.

I ignore it, intent on finding a decent inn to spend the night.

A door swings open, and a group of men stumble from a worn threshold, laughing at one another. One man, still holding a bottle of sharply scented wine, trips. He stumbles backwards into a friend of his, dark liquid splashing over the sides of the bottle, staining the cobblestone. A bitter, pungent smell fills the air, and I wrinkle my nose.

Alwyne whinnies disapprovingly, shaking his mane. I lean over, patting his neck gingerly, a silent agreement. I urge him on, past the men, eager to avoid them.

"Hey!"

My hands tighten about the reins, ignoring the man's call.

"Yer there!"

I bring Alwyne to a halt, tilting my head to the sky and letting my eyes flutter closed as I take a steadying breath, agitation churning my stomach.

Cautiously, I cock my head so that I may see the men, who have approached my side, their wary eyes on Alwyne as they maintain their distance.

"Something I can help you with?" I ask, feigning politeness.

The man at the head of the group raises his bottle, bleary eyes settling on my satchel as the liquid sloshes onto the cobblestones.

"If you plan on robbing me, I suggest you be more subtle about it."

The man tips his head to the side, reaching out with the bottle to point at my satchel. Then, he stumbles forward a few steps, halting at my side so that he can lean forward to inspect the buckle.

Alwyne whinnies, and I allow my hand to drop to the hilt of my dagger in warning. He seems to notice the movement, despite his drunken state, and takes a step back, not removing his eyes from my satchel.

"Got a frien' Clara. Had er orse' stolen a lil while ago. Got them same..." he trails off, waving his hand at the buckles on my satchel.

"They are called buckles, and had you been sober, I may have sympathised with your friend, but in your state, I do not believe you shall know the difference between an apple and a carrot were they to be thrown at you, so I suggest you head home before you can trouble yourself or others."

Clicking my tongue, I urge Alwyne into a slow trot, eager to be rid of these men, who continue to call after me. It is not long until their shouts fade into the night.

A while later, I spot a small inn. It is set at the corner of a faintly illuminated street. Outside there is a sign, *Vacancies*, it reads.

In this part of the village, it is quieter. Nobody roams the streets, and I am free to slide off Alwyne. My eyes scan the space around me, searching for a safe place to tie him.

I startle, caught off guard by a cat. It scurries from the darkness of a building, its fur so dark it blends into the night. Its eyes glow an eerie yellow as it casts me a glance. Then, it scampers into a shadowed alley.

Releasing a breath, the tension leaves my body. Momentarily.

I brush my hand over the bridge of Alwyne's nose yet remain distracted. My gaze follows the cat's path from where it emerged to the alley it vanished within. There, hidden in the shadows, is a worn fence. It curves around the side of the building, disappearing into the darkness. Only a part of it is visible from the street.

I lead Alwyne over, hand falling to the hilt of my dagger. I narrow my eyes, investigating the dark side street. There are no signs of imminent danger, and so I tie Alwyne to the post, leaving him to graze on the small patch of grass and stray bucket of water. I return to the street.

The inn is not extravagant. With two stories, it offers no reassurance in its stability. The windows are dusty and bordered with black shutters, most curtains are drawn, and occasionally, a shadow flits by. The garden is small, with dead flowers resting beneath the windows. Like the rest, the structure is tilted, hovering over me in a wordless threat.

I start towards the door, hood up, protection against both the wind and unwanted company. The handle is rusted, coarse against my palm. It slips as I turn it, threatening to break off.

The door creaks, announcing my entrance.

I step into a narrow corridor. The walls are lined with hooks, and a crooked sign hangs above the arched doorway. *The Filly*, it reads. Noise erupts through the threshold.

Adjusting my hood to shield my face, I tread into the next room.

Immediately, I am met with the obnoxious atmosphere of a village bar. The room curves around the doorway in an awkward, boxy U-shape. The walls are made of dark wood, paired with a few candles. There is a single chandelier, yet the candles within give off nothing more than a feeble orange glow. Around me, the crowded room bustles with people. They laugh obnoxiously loud, bottles of dark liquid sloshing about their hands. Tables are overturned, and chairs lay waste around the room, their legs snapped and ripped apart.

Most are too inebriated to care.

I wrinkle my nose at the smell, spiced and heavy. Too strong. Carefully, I make my way toward the back of the room, dodging stray bottles of wine or a poorly aimed punch. Disgust draws my features, yet I am careful to hide it.

Skimming around the bar, I slip through a threshold on the right wall, escaping the boisterous room.

There is a small wooden table. A single candle rests atop its worn surface, complimented by a stack of books, their spines cracked and worn. Their edges are peeling away, and the words are faded.

"Can I help ya?"

My eyes flicker to the woman behind the desk.

She sits hunched over on a wooden stool, her hazel hair falling in soft waves over her shoulders, highlighted with a few streaks of blonde. When her gaze meets mine, I see her eyes, the palest of blue, piercing and impatient. She taps her nails against the desk, short and chewed, awaiting my answer.

"I would like a room for the night, please."

She wrinkles her nose, looking me up and down.

"I'm afraid we're all out."

I deflate at her words. This is the quietest place I could find. I do not wish to risk myself to find another place where danger is sure to be more prominent.

"You must have *one* room," I insist. "You cannot deny the sign outside."

Her lips twist, and she scowls at me. "I don't lie."

I raise my eyebrows, reaching for the gold coins given to me by Alistar. I flip one in the air, letting my gaze return to the women. "I would be happy to find another place to spend my pay."

She halts her tapping, eyes widening. After a moment of silence, she shakes her head, wiping away her shock. She narrows her eyes at me.

"Ya will have to pay mor' an that."

A startled, aggravated sound escapes me. "*More?*"

Anger bubbling in my stomach, I step up to the desk, placing my palms against the rough wood. Leaning forward, my hood falls away from my face. When I whisper, it is menacing.

"I do not believe you know the value of these coins. If you wish to stand here and banter over the worth of one of your measly rooms, I will gladly find someplace else. I am sure your master would love to hear how you lost such great pay."

She bites her lip and, after a moment, opens her mouth to speak.

"That will not be necessary," a male voice echoes.

I turn, straightening myself as a man steps up beside me, throwing an arm around my shoulders.

"It would be my pleasure to cover the cost. Name your price," he says, a grin splitting his lips.

Jerking away from him, I step out of his reach. Leaning back, my features draw with disgust.

"I—"

"Surprised, are you?" he asks.

I stare at him, brows pinched. There is something familiar about his teasing tone, the playful air about him. He stares back, eyebrows raised. His hair is a defined copper, framing his sharp features and high cheekbones. Mesmerising hazel eyes, flecked with shimmering gold, are locked on mine. Confusion grips me.

Then, a realisation dawns on me, and the air is squeezed from my lungs.

Ofen.

One of my closest childhood friends. We met in Enia, his home kingdom, when I used to visit frequently. That was before the death of my father. I have not seen him since I was a child.

A grin splits my lips.

Ofen returns my joy, his lips curving into a grin. Without hesitation, I step up to him, drawing him into an embrace. He wraps his arms around me, returning the gesture.

"It took you long enough," he whispers. He is slightly taller than I, closer to that of Killian's height, and must bend forward so that only I alone can hear the words.

A quiet laugh bubbles in my throat, and I close my eyes against his chest, allowing myself this small sense of comfort—a reassurance in the dark maze of my mind.

I cannot believe that after all these years, we have found each other again.

Cannot believe he remembers me.

I have changed a lot since we were children.

I break away from him, suddenly aware of the woman's curious gaze.

"How did you recognise me?"

His lips curve into a grin. "You are not easily forgettable, Thalia, but it was your eyes. The moment I saw them, I knew who stood before me."

I beam in response. "What brings you to Verila?" I ask, a thousand questions bubbling up my throat.

"We will have plenty of time to talk." He looks me up and down, his eyebrows quirking at my battered state. "Once you are able to make yourself presentable."

I scoff. "Kind as always, Ofen."

He lays an arm across his stomach, dropping into a bow. "Milady."

I roll my eyes, and he straightens, a smile curling his lips, brilliant and unwavering. He slaps a bundle of coins onto the desk with an air of arrogance. "One room for the lady, please."

The woman behind the desk stares at the pouch for a moment, eyebrows pinched. Then she swipes them into her greedy hands, and they disappear into her pocket. Ofen raises his brows yet says nothing. She hastily hands over a key.

"Up those stairs," she says. A scrawny finger points to the stairwell behind me.

"Find me when you are ready," Ofen speaks. He lays a hand on my shoulder, meeting my gaze. "It is good to see you, Thalia."

My lips curve into a smile. "As it is you."

His hand falls away, and he takes a step back, disappearing into the other room. He vanishes into the crowd.

I turn to the stairs, surveying them carefully. A few of the boards are split, with sharp protruding edges. Carefully, I make my way up them, wincing as they creak beneath my weight, threatening to snap.

At the top, there is a narrow corridor branching off to either side of me. I turn left, scanning the hall as I go. It is dark, lit only by a few measly torches. The flames dance across the dusty walls, highlighting the cracks. A cockroach scuttles by my feet.

I halt at my door, looking it over. A frown tugs at my lips, and I slip the key into the rusted lock. It clicks, and I push the door open, stepping inside.

The room is small. There is a single bed tucked into the corner of the room, complete with thread-bare sheets and a thin pillow. Beside it, there is a cabinet, a dusty candelabra upon it. I catch a glimpse of my reflection staring back at me from a full-size mirror. On the other side is a tub, barely large enough for one person. A towel is draped over the side.

It is far from luxurious, yet it holds the necessities, and that is all I need.

I tread over to the bed, swinging off my cloak and tossing it onto the worn sheets. Unsheathing my daggers, I lay them on the cabinet. Their blades remain covered in dried blood, a reminder of my last battle. I lean my bow and quiver against the wall. Then, quietly, I make for the door, exiting my temporary quarters to amble back down the precarious steps.

I halt at the desk, waiting for the woman to catch sight of me, yet she is too focused on her shiny new coins to notice.

I clear my throat, and her head snaps up.

"I would like some water, please, for the bath."

Her eyebrows crease, thin lips tugging into a frown.

"I'll send someon' up."

I step away, bowing my head as I restrain my annoyance with her discontent. "Thank you."

She does not reply, gaze returning to the valuable coins tucked into the folds of her tattered garments.

Deciding to return to my quarters, I skip up the steps and down the dank corridor, slipping back into the room.

While I wait, I pad back over to the mirror, surveying my reflection. For the most part, my face is clean, free of blood and dirt. Yet there is a cut on my cheek, a perfect, straight line. Barely noticeable. I run my hands gently along the leather of my dress, which hangs just above the knees over a pair of dark pants. I brush off the dirt, frowning at the mud on my boots.

I suppose Ofen is right. I am not as presentable as one would hope.

Not long after my trip downstairs, my attention is caught by a knock at the door, short and abrupt. Instantly tense, I tread to the door, caution written in my steps.

It seems my trust is waning.

Carefully, I let my fingers close over the handle, twisting it open until I catch sight of a young boy. I release a breath, body sagging as the tension leaves me.

The child is young, scrawny, looking to be barely older than seven. His greasy black hair drapes to either side of his face, covering his eyes and framing his gaunt features, hollow cheeks and pale lips.

I open the door wider, surprised by the smile that curves my lips. It is genuine, despite the odd twist my heart gives.

It pains me to see one of such a young age so disconnected and lifeless.

Without a word, the boy saunters into my room, over to the tub, and lifts a bucket over his head, skeletal arms quivering with the weight of it. Water splashes into the tub, sloshing up the sides and staining the wooden floorboards.

Then, he turns, scampering through the doorway to refill his bucket.

I want to offer my assistance, to do it myself, but never once does he acknowledge me. I attempt to speak to him, to offer my aid, yet he does nothing but drift past me, eyes shallow, unseeing.

He does not acknowledge my presence.

Does not speak a word when I smile at him nor when I try to make conversation to break the strenuous silence.

After a while, I give in.

Resting on the edge of the bed, I can do nothing but watch the boy tread back and forth, arms trembling as he pours bucket after bucket. When he leaves the room once more, I pad back over to the tub to check its depth, lacing my fingers together when I find it is less than half full. With a resigned breath, I decide to occupy myself, yet I find myself constantly glancing his way, concern creasing my brows, until finally, he leaves my quarters, closing the door behind him.

He does not return after that.

# ELEVEN
## THALIA

y the time the tub is filled, I have cleaned my daggers free of blood, polished my boots to a shine, and treated and re-wrapped the wound on my upper arm.

The rug is rough beneath my feet; its once soft, fluffy fabric now worn and ragged. My hand finds the edge of the tub as I lean over it, dipping a finger into the water to test its temperature. Tepid.

Carefully, I climb in, sinking slowly into the water. It warms my body, soothing my tired muscles and aching limbs. There is a jug set on a small table beside the tub. I plunge it into the water, watching bubbles form on the surface as it fills. Then, I pour it over my head, rinsing my hair and untangling the knotted strands.

When my hair is clean, I set the jug back on the table, scrubbing the remaining grime from my body. Then, gripping the sides of the tub. I sink beneath the surface, closing my eyes. The water rushes over me, enveloping me in a warm embrace. For a moment, it washes all the pain away. Washes away my fears and my worries. It frees my mind of thoughts. It relieves the dull pounding at the back of my head.

It erases every thought of my failure.

Every thought of Killian.

I breach the surface, gasping for air. My vision is blurry, and I bring my hands to my eyes, hastily wiping away the water. I blink, taking in my surroundings.

And everything comes crashing back to me.

My chest feels heavier than before, and I am stuck with the burden of my troubles, my emotions.

A low, frustrated sound escapes my lips, yet it is partly a sob. I bite my lip, hard enough to draw blood, angered by my own weakness.

Fighting a rush of emotion, I stand abruptly. Swinging my leg over the edge of the tub and landing on the jaded rug. I wring my hair out, then jerk the towel off the table, wrapping it tightly around my body.

I stalk over to the bed, drying myself with a sense of ire. Tossing the towel over the bedpost, I pull my clothes back on, not bothering with my bracers. When I am done, I step in front of the mirror. My hair remains damp, yet it falls in smooth, straight strands down my back, complemented by the curls at the end. Now, my eyes are brighter; my lashes flecked with water. I have left no traces of the recent days—my struggles and endurances. No blood nor dirt remains on my body, and my wound is treated and wrapped properly.

On the outside, I am but a mere village girl—a commoner. I look unharmed and tranquil. I look as if I have endured no hardships, as though I have suffered no significant wounds nor seen a kingdom and everybody in it burn.

I look as though I have not lost my best friend.

The man that matters most to me.

The man that is *everything* to me.

The man that has always been there for me, no matter what I was going through. Who treated me like his equal, despite our separate roles and status.

*Love makes fools of us all.*

Yes. I suppose it does.

# TWELVE
## KILLIAN

hen I awaken, the sun has slipped beyond the trees, replaced by the silver glow of the moon.

I roll my head to the side, groggy. My eyes flutter open, and I blink a few times, gaining my bearings. The forest is dim, lit only by the shimmer of stars and moon above. Slowly, I climb to my feet, stretching my arms above my head.

To my side, Elwis whinnies.

A tentative smile curls my lips, and I find my way to her, bringing a hand beneath her mane.

"Are you ready to ride?"

In response, she drops her head, sniffing the forest floor. I pat her neck lightly, not expecting a response.

Although I am not fully rested, the sleep I have gained is enough to rid me of the overwhelming exhaustion I had felt earlier.

Before mounting, I take hold of the berries in my satchel, popping a few into my mouth before tying the pouch. Deeper in the valley, I should be able to replenish them, yet there are few left, and I cannot afford to waste them.

I pull myself onto Elwis's back. She whinnies, throwing her head

73

back, and I reach down, patting her neck lightly. I squeeze her sides, and we depart the forest, struggling upon the uneven forest floor. Once we are back onto the rugged shoreline, we continue towards Enia.

Although my stomach still rumbles, I have eaten enough to summon my strength. For now, I must worry only about the necessities. Once I reach Lsthrain, I may eat until I can eat no more. I may recover from the recent, tiresome days, the heartache and the pain.

At that, my argument with Thalia washes over me once more.

A wide, yawning chasm opens in the pit of my stomach, and I feel an emptiness unlike anything I have felt before. It spreads within me a horrible, impenetrable darkness, swallowing everything inside of me. It leaves nothing but the pain—the harsh ache of an unyielding regret.

Everything hurts.

The beat of my heart is nothing more than a steady rhythm of my guilt, slamming painfully against my chest, heavy with longing.

*How?* I wonder. *How* could I have said those things to her? To my best friend since childhood?

No, so much more.

Thalia, who I have trained with, laughed with, cried with? Thalia, who has comforted me as I comforted her?

Thalia, who has supported me as I supported her?

How could I hurt her after everything she has been through? All the pain and hurt she has suffered in her life? How could *I*, her *best friend*, hurt her still? Knowing full well how much she was already hurting, *especially* after recent days?

Because you do not always realise the value of something, or *someone* until they are gone.

But I did. I did realise her value, but I still allowed my cold heart to best me.

I have abandoned her, just as her parents did when they died. Just as Calivar did when he went down with his kingdom.

And yet she means more to me than anybody could possibly comprehend.

I slam my hand down onto my saddle, nails digging hard into the leather. I catch my lip between my teeth, biting with enough force to draw blood. Yet the pain is nothing; it is distant.

I deserve so much worse for what I have done.

She has every right to hate me.

But *Elders*, I hope she does not.

I should not have left. I should not have left on such terms. Not any time, but especially in times such as these. I do not know what will happen today nor tomorrow. I do not know whether I will see the next sunrise or sunset. I do not know if I will live to see her again. If I will live to apologise for everything I have said.

To tell her how I feel.

What a fool I have been, too overcome by my fear to express myself.

There is so much I want to say. *So. Much.*

So much I might never get to say.

I miss her. I miss her more than I have ever missed anybody.

A low, rumbling sound erupts from my right, drawing me from my thoughts.

I bring Elwis to a halt, one hand tightening upon the reins whilst the other flies to the hilt of my dagger. I narrow my eyes, leaning forward to squint into the darkness of a cave, which is engraved into the base of one of Enia's mountains.

Orange light flickers across the walls of the hollow, and another growl follows the first.

Fear grips my aching heart, and without thinking, I slip from Elwis's back. I wait a moment, listening to the silence, deafening in its suspense. When I hear nor see anything, I lead Elwis to a dark patch of bushes set at the foot of the mountains, a short distance from the cave. I rub her nose gently, a silent gesture of assurance, then slip along the cold stone, back pressed against the hard surface, silent as I tread over the pebbles.

I stop at the entrance of the cave, both the sheet of darkness and towering stone walls acting as my cover. Peering around the corner, I search the blackness, the shadows dancing on the tunnel walls, yet they reveal nothing.

And so I draw my daggers, adjusting their cool gold hilts in my hands. Then, I slip into the cave, pressing myself against the wall. Ahead, there are voices, distant and low. Rumbling.

There is no mistaking to whom they belong.

I edge along the wall, careful to remain silent. As I continue, the voices grow louder, rising above the crackle of a fire. Despite their raised voices, I cannot discern their words. They speak in a language I cease to understand.

I halt at a bend, angling myself to peer around the wall. There, in a small cavern, are a horde of racai.

My lungs constrict.

The beasts are gathered about a raging fire, weapons and armour strewn across the stone floor—the fresh blood upon the armour's surface glints. My stomach turns, fear bubbling up my throat.

It hurts to think about whom that blood may have belonged to.

A shout echoes from the cavern, and one of the beasts stands, hauling one of its companions from its seat on the stone. The racai slams its accomplice against the wall, which quakes beneath the brute's strength. The first to stand is abnormally large, with bulging muscles that run the expanse of its broad shoulders and chest. It towers over the smaller beast, which is pressed against the cold stone, teeth bared.

"Careful," the brute growls, bunching up the threadbare shirt of the racai, who squirms, trying to free itself from the chief's grasp. "You would not wish to ruin our plans, would you? Our alliance with the trolls is sealed; the elves do not stand a chance against our battalion. If you do not wish to further hinder us, I suggest you keep your mouth shut before I do it for you."

The victim squirms once more, wrinkled features curved into a wince. When the brute does not relinquish his hold, the smaller racai gives in, sagging against the wall. Its face twists into a sneer, yet its surrender is clear. Reluctantly, the chief releases the beast, allowing it to drop to the hard ground. A growl passes the brute's lips as it turns, returning to its place by the fire.

They return to their conversation, words exchanged in harsh tones, one only followers of Sindir shall understand.

*The elves do not stand a chance against our battalion.*

At that, I feel all my fear wash away. In its place, a rush of sizzling rage makes my hands quiver, and I curl my fingers impossibly tighter about my daggers. A muscle leaps in my jaw.

Movement from the side of the cavern catches my attention, and I watch as the lesser racai stands, his red eyes never leaving its leader. They flash with barely contained fury. Rubbing its arm, it turns, marching away from the group.

Towards me.

I whirl around, searching the darkness for a place to hide.

A little way down, I spot a crevice, barely wide enough to squeeze through.

I must take my chances.

Trained in the skills of survival, I slide soundlessly along the wall. Without a choice, I wedge my body between the stone, holding my breath as the rock closes around me, sharp edges digging into my chest and back. My features curve into a wince as I slide further into the shadows.

The beast's footfalls echo, ricocheting off the stone wall. It storms past without so much as a glance in my direction.

I release a breath, the tension momentarily leaving my body. When the footsteps have faded, I squeeze between the walls, then suck in a sharp breath as I slip free, back into the dim tunnel.

I examine my surroundings, listening for the horde of racai as I expect them to grow closer, their weapons drawn and voices raised.

Yet they do not come. They remain within the cavern, no care towards their companion, who has vanished from their sights.

My lips quirk towards a smile.

Warily, I tread back towards the cave's entrance, daggers brandished. Halting at the opening, I remain within the shadows, concealed from the racai's view. It stands at the river's edge, back to me, with a small, curved dagger in hand. It is significantly smaller than my own and shall be no hardship to pry away.

Allowing one dagger back into my sheath, I step free of the tunnel, inching towards the beast. My footfalls are silent, despite the pebbles beneath my feet. Years of training have taught me how to move unnoticed.

Now close enough to see the monster's features, distinct in the silver moonlight, I lunge.

I have the racai in my hold before it can react.

Its body jerks, trying desperately to escape my grasp, yet my hold is too tight, my strength too great. With one arm about the racai's throat, the other held over its mouth, I drag it towards the forest.

The beast is persistent, struggling against my hold, yet I do not yield. When we reach the wood, I haul it out of sight, and the racai digs its feet into the dirt to slow our progress.

Its sharp teeth sink into my forearm.

Pain lances through my limb as my flesh is torn and fresh blood wells on my arm. I bare my teeth against the pain, a grunt passing my lips. Still, I do not release the beast.

Its violence only angers me further.

As soon as we are out of sight, I slam the beast against a tree.

It hisses through its bared teeth, jagged and stained permanently with blood.

"You *imbecile—*" I snarl, jabbing my elbow into the racai's throat. Blood trickles down my arm, burning alongside the fury coiling in my stomach. "I suppose this is new to you. Never been the victim, have you? Always killing the innocent, torturing and burning, acting without mercy. You do not know how it feels to be on a side where it seems there is no hope, to be a part of a losing battle. You do not know how it feels to be beaten and tortured without reason, to lose everything you hold dear." I lean closer so that our faces are mere inches apart. "I will *make* sure you know how it feels."

The beast wriggles, face screwed up, eyes wide. Its efforts are futile. I am easily a head and a half taller, my chest and shoulders far broader and more powerful.

"Tell me your plans. Tell me how you wish to approach Lsthrain and how you shall breach it."

The racai only struggles more.

"*Dammit,*" I growl, pressing my elbow further into the racai's throat. I place my blade at its stomach, letting the tip nick its charred skin.

It gasps, clutching at my arm, its nails digging into my skin as it tries to pry me away, yet succeeds only in provoking me further.

Without a thought, I slam the blade into the beast's gut.

A wretched cry escapes its thin lips, and blood pours from the wound, staining the ground at my feet.

My limbs quiver with fury.

"You *see?*" I spit. "You see what it is to be at the mercy of your enemy?" I twist my blade up through its ribcage. "You see what it is to feel *pain?*"

I drive my blade through the beast's heart.

Its lips part, jaw slack with shock. Then the light fades from its eyes and its body sags.

My vision blurs, tears welling behind my eyes. Tears of rage and pain and all the hurt I have been hiding and forcing away.

I step away, jerking my dagger free.

Its body falls to the ground with a soft thud.

Then, overwhelmed by emotion, I whirl, sending my blade through the air with an angered cry, the dagger lodges into the trunk of a nearby tree, rocking violently from the force of my throw.

I slump against a tree, resting my forehead against the rough bark. It digs into my skin, yet I do not care. I pound the trunk with my fist, eyes squeezed shut. Over and over, I slam my fists against the tree, the rough grooves carving into my flesh until I can no longer bear the sting, and my knuckles come away bloody.

I sink down against the trunk, burying my face in my palms. They are raw and stained with my crystal-red blood, and my arm echoes with the pain of the racai's bite. I take no care, ignoring the constant gush of blood, the simmering pain.

I am such a fool.

Again, I have let my anger better me. The beast had valuable information. I could have pressed it further. I could have learnt of their plans, how they will breach Lsthrain, and how many are in their battalion.

Instead, I killed the beast.

And I am no better for it.

There are more of them, yet I cannot risk going into their cavern. I cannot pull another beast away unnoticed.

*So weak.*

*So cold.*

*So cruel.*

*Like my father.*

"There."

I jerk my head up, hand flying to my dagger. Pain lances through my forearm, yet it is nothing. Nothing compared to the hot spike of fear that builds in my gut.

Beyond the tree line, caught in the silver streaks of moonlight, the horde of racai stands.

Their weapons are brandished, the orange glow of their torches flickering in my direction, penetrating the shadows I cower within.

A malicious grin twists the corner of the chief's mouth, and it spins its sword about its hand.

Then they charge.

# THIRTEEN
## THALIA

hen I arrive downstairs, the bar is rowdier than before. The scent of wine hangs heavy in the air, burning my nostrils. Shattered glass lay strewn across the floor, dark liquid staining the wooden boards and seeping into the cracks.

I scan the room for Ofen, yet the crowd is too thick. There are too many people, too many broken chairs and overturned tables. I squeeze between people, narrowly avoiding a misguided punch or a loosely thrown bottle. They glare at me as I slip between them, and my features curve to return their scowls.

It is loud. The dull pounding in my head heightens to a hammering, and I grimace. Squeezing between people, I spot Ofen. He sits in a dimly lit corner, drink in hand. I release an aggravated breath, making my way towards him, eager to free myself from these people.

Somebody staggers into me, and I stumble forward, crashing into a nearby table. Glasses tip, and a sharp, spiced scent reaches my nose. The men at the table shout, their enraged voices rising over the chaos. I push myself away from the table as one of the men stands, staring down at me with dangerous brown eyes. His shoulders are as broad as two men, and he is abnormally tall, allowing him to tower over me.

"Careful," the man hisses. "It'd be easy for a weak little lady to get hurt, specially' in a place like this."

I fight back a remark, a bubble of rage forming in my stomach. I do not like his assumption that I am *weak*.

"That is rather presumptuous."

Ire flickers across his features, his eyes flashing threateningly. Eager not to linger, I turn, making for the crowd. Before I can get anywhere, he grabs my hair, jerking me toward him until my back hits his chest. I bite back a cry.

"I would be careful if I were you. You never know who may have a weapon hidden up their sleeve," he whispers against my ear, a warning beneath his tone. From afar, it will look like nothing more than a gesture of affection, yet here, his threat is clear. He whirls me to face him, and I glance at his sleeve, where I see the familiar glint of a blade.

Yet I do not heed his words, for I do not fear him, nor his blade. He can do nothing to me in a place as public as this.

I have had years of training and do not need another to protect me, to remove me from harm's way.

The corners of my lips twitch, and I raise my chin, smirking. I meet his gaze, eyebrows raised pompously.

"Indeed." Gently, I flick the edge of my cloak aside, revealing the gold hilt of my dagger. It is much larger than the measly thing in the man's sleeve.

His eyes widen, shock breaking his composure. Then, they narrow, flickering up to meet my gaze.

"You will come to regret that," he snarls.

I raise my eyebrows. "Will I?"

Without another word, I jerk free of his grasp, slipping through the crowd to Ofen's table.

"Ah, there you are."

I slide onto the cushioned bench, taking the side opposite of him. The cushion is worn, a slit in the edge allowing the feathers to spill out beneath my weight.

"You look much better," he says.

"Is that a compliment?"

His lips quirk into a smile, offering no response.

I tilt my head, motioning to his glass. "Save me the troubles of your inebriation. Tell me you are not yet drunk?"

He laughs, a rich, hearty sound. "I am not. Nor will I be."

"Mhm." I lay my hands on the table, weaving my fingers together. "I would hope not," I mutter.

My mood is already low, anger bubbling in my stomach, ready to boil over at the slightest inconvenience. I do not need a drunk Ofen to further hinder me.

"Drinks?"

A woman has appeared at my side. She wears a simple, tattered dress with loose stitches and fraying fabric. Her hair is thrown into a messy braided bun, and she carries a tray of overflowing glasses.

Ofen raises his glass, swirling the remaining liquid before he throws it back, then sets it down with a dramatic thud.

"Two more, please, and something to eat for my friend," he requests.

She nods, grabbing his glass before hurrying off.

"It would seem you have made a friend, Thalia," Ofen chimes, a question in his voice.

I raise my eyebrows.

He smirks, then motions to the table I bumped into.

"I presume you bought that man another drink, no? You did, after all, spill them. *All* of them."

I scoff. "Please, I do not waste my coins on men such as them, nor any, for that matter."

He lifts his eyebrows, and I return the gesture. He drops his head, releasing a breath.

"What happened over there? If I did not know better, it would seem you got into a bit of a quibble."

"A quibble, if you will," I mutter. Casting a glance across the room, I notice the men's absence, their spilt drinks left in their wake. I narrow my eyes.

"He did not hurt you, did he?"

"No. No, he did not. He merely threatened me. Yet it was empty; one cannot be so foolish as to draw a knife in such a public area." A smug smile curls my lips, vanishing as quickly as it had formed. My mind drifts to my argument with Killian. The harsh words we exchanged, too caught up in the moment to consider the words before we spoke them aloud.

*Love makes fools of us all.*

Elders, I hate him.

I hate him for what he said. I hate him for choosing me over Valindor.

"Men can be so foolish," I breathe.

I am met with silence.

After a moment, Ofen speaks, his voice soft: "You should be careful, especially around men like him. You could get hurt."

I bring my gaze to his, and I feel my rage spike, feel it climb up my throat.

"And why is that? Because you do not think I can handle myself? Because you remember me as the innocent, sensitive young girl? *Elders.*" I lean back in my chair, nails digging into the wooden table. "I have *changed.* I am no longer the girl you remember. I do not beg for the mercy of those who are more powerful than I, and I sure as *hell* do not need anybody's protection. *I* can take care of *myself.*"

Ofen stares at me, his eyes shimmering with flecks of gold. They hold my gaze with an undeniable softness, and I fight the fury burning up my throat. I do not want his pity.

"Elders, Thalia. What has the world done to you?" His voice is delicate, sympathetic.

At that, I deflate. Swallowing hard, I wrap my arms around myself and avert my gaze. I feel myself begin to tremble, tears building behind my eyes as pressure mounts in my chest.

*I will not cry.*

"Too much," I whisper.

For the next little while, we sit in silence.

Again, I am left alone with my emotions. Alone with the thoughts of everything I have left behind. Everything and *everyone* I have lost.

And I cannot take it.

"So," I say, clearing my voice. "What brings you here, to Verila?"

Ofen hesitates.

"My travels. I plan to reach Thilia soon, yet I hear rumours of beasts on the prowl. It is nothing like the average beast, one of which you might find in the forest or the dark dwelling of a cave. I have heard of something much more bloodthirsty than your regular troll. I did not think it wise to travel through the night."

The woman returns with two glasses, full to the brim with frothy liquid, and a plate of bread and cheese balanced on her arm. She sets the glasses on the table with exaggerated force, and dark yellow liquid sloshes up the sides, fizzing as it hits the table. She slides the plate into the centre of the table, then scurries off without a word.

Ofen takes his glass, raising it to his lips. When he sets it down, he wraps his hands around the glass, tapping quietly against it.

"I do not believe those stories, of course. I will not take the word of cowards."

I cock my head as I reach for a piece of cheese, which is long past its best. "I would advise rethinking your beliefs," I say, popping the cheese in my mouth before grasping my glass. I take a small sip, grimacing as the liquid passes my lips. It is unlike anything I have tasted before. Sour on my tongue, it leaves a herby, bitter residue.

"And why is that?" He questions, undeterred.

"Because I have seen them myself."

For a moment, he is silent. And then his lips curve into a grin, and he begins to chuckle.

My stomach twists aggressively, and I slam my glass onto the table. He falls quiet.

"I am glad to see you have not lost your trust in me," I hiss.

Ofen winces, mouthing opening, then closing. "Thalia, I—"

"They brought down Enia."

He freezes.

"You must be mistaken," he utters, yet his voice has an unmistakable twinge of fear.

"No," I shake my head. I wish I could deny it. Wish I could say that it is not true. Say that I am merely playing some sick joke.

And yet, that is what it is, is it not?

Everything.

All my loss. My parents. Grimsmith. Calivar. Enia. Valindor.

Killian.

All some sick joke.

*If only it were.*

"If only I were."

He slumps back in his seat, chest rising and falling slowly, painfully. His eyes close, and he runs a hand through his long copper hair, which falls past his shoulders, an inch or two longer than Killian's.

"How can you know this?"

I hesitate, reaching for a slice of bread, which is days old and hard. It crunches as I bite into it, and I wince. "Because I saw it."

When he offers no response, I lean forward, lowering my voice so that only he may hear.

"Enia will not be the last, Ofen. They have returned. I have encountered them myself, the racai and the Blood Riders. "

He shakes his head, running a hand down his face.

"*Elders,*" he breathes. "Why, Thalia? Why have they returned?"

I do not respond.

"Thalia," he repeats, straightening himself. His gaze has turned hard.

"They want Valindor. They *have* Valindor," I correct, so that only he may hear.

"No. Valindor was lost."

"*Was.*"

He drops his head into his hands. "You are telling me that the racai have discovered Valindor's location and hence retrieved it?"

I bite my lip. "Something like that, I suppose."

"'*Something like that?*'" he snarls. "Tell me what you mean, Thalia. I am not one for riddles."

I narrow my eyes, nails sinking into the wood. "Not here, Ofen."

"Tomorrow, then."

"I cannot linger here. Tomorrow I must continue my travels."

His jaw clenches, and he averts his gaze, anger flashing in his eyes. "Where do you head that calls for such haste?"

"Orathin."

"*Orathin?*" He echoes, eyes flicking back to mine. "Why in the h—"
Ofen releases a breath, an incredulous grin splitting his lips. "I suppose you cannot explain that either, can you?"

"No, I cannot."

His hands fall to the table, and he pushes himself to his feet. He leans forward, a vein pulsing in his neck.

"Tomorrow, we ride together, and you will tell me *everything*."

I have not the time to argue, for he is gone before the words can leave my lips.

# FOURTEEN
## KILLIAN

anic lances through me, and I shoot to my feet, rapidly moving to draw my daggers, yet only one remains in its sheath.

The other remains lodged in the tree.

I curse myself, eyes sweeping wildly over my surroundings, mind reeling as I desperately try to procure a plan.

The racai are close now. Too close.

With no other choice, my hand flies to an arrow tipped by the scale of a dragon. As soon as my bow hits my hand, I nock the arrow into place, firing at the onslaught of beasts. Their bodies drop two, three, four down. I continue to fire, round after round, as they approach, the curve of my bow familiar against my palm, the movement practised, effortless.

Despite the handful I have killed, they still outnumber me.

Their roars echo in the darkness, closing in on me from all sides, squeezing the air from my lungs as fear ripples through my gut. Now, they are far too close to continue my onslaught of arrows. Their heavy footfalls thud against the earth as I draw my remaining dagger, bow cast over my shoulder.

My blade clashes with that of a racai, sending a flurry of sparks into

the night, and pain tears through the bite wound, making me grunt. I
duck beneath the sword, spinning to thrust my dagger into the stomach
of another beast, then drop into a roll to avoid decapitation. With a few
swipes of my blade, I take two down, using their bodies to shield myself
against the brute's blow. Blood splatters my pauldron, my face, my
hair, and I swipe the back of my arm across my face. Yet it only makes
it worse, the blood from the gash remaining and the sting worsening.
Blood smears my face, obscuring my vision.

It is enough to make me falter.

The racai slams into me, and I stagger back, tripping over a log. It
sends me sprawling, and I land hard in the dirt, the air knocked from my
lungs. I cough, sucking in a sharp breath, yet no air enters.

Scrambling backwards in the soil, I keep my blade steady in my hand.
The racai moves towards me, painstakingly slow. Its charred lips are
twisted into a malicious grin, a symbol of its enjoyment.

I propel myself onto my feet, barreling forwards into the beast. We
stagger back, the force of my movement throwing us both off balance. I
brandish my blade, gritting my teeth as I stand before the racai, my fists
and forearm throbbing painfully.

A roar emits from the beast's throat, and it tosses its sword into the
opposite hand, staring me down.

Then it lunges.

With a swift movement, I spin around the blade, blood flying from
my wound as I do so. I draw my dagger over the exposed skin at the back
of its neck. The beast howls, swinging for my abdomen. I leap out of its

reach, swiping for its legs, yet a wave of dizziness catches me off guard, and I miscalculate.

And miss.

I fall back against a tree. The rough trunk digs into my back, and I struggle to regain my breath.

A gleam catches my eye, and I tilt my head back, catching sight of my dagger lodged into the wood beside my head.

The racai continue to advance.

Ten, plus the leader, who is far larger and more robust than the rest.

I stand no chance.

Not here. Not with an exposed wound that continues to seep crystal blood, which is now staining my flesh, the fabric of my shirt. Not with the blood I have lost. Not with the dizziness and sudden exhaustion crashing over me, making the world tilt and blur before me. Not with the nausea stirring in the pit of my stomach.

With no choice, I rip my dagger from the wood, gritting my teeth against nausea and pain. Then I slam it into the wood again, higher this time, using it to propel myself onto a branch just out of the racai's reach.

The beasts erupt into a frenzy of enraged howls, their weapons raised towards me, the blood on their blades glinting in the silver starlight. They curse in a language I do not understand, yet their threat is clear, taunting me, trying to tempt me into leaving the branch, into fighting them.

Their advantage is evident, as is my weakness, and they know should I fight them now, their victory will be inevitable.

They want to see me suffer.

But I already am.

I sag against the trunk, daggers in hand, breaths ragged, unsteady. *Painful.* My stomach coils, and I feel the familiar rolling of nausea in my belly, bile clawing up my throat. I clutch my stomach to keep from retching, my vision blurring from the restraint and loss of blood.

My arm is soaked in warm, sticky blood.

A deep, rounded gash is carved into my forearm, the surrounding skin pierced by sharp teeth marks. A chunk of my flesh has been ripped out, and the excruciating throb of the wound refuses to dissipate.

If I cannot treat it soon, I shall bleed out.

I sway towards the edge yet quickly jolt back to my senses and catch myself on the trunk before I can plummet into the racai's eager arms.

Below me, they cackle.

I bite my lip against the pain, tilting my head back with an anguished groan. Placing a hand over the slit to stem the bleeding, the hurt intensifies, and a startled cry escapes my lips. I curse myself for being so weak.

An arrow skims past me.

I recoil suddenly, caught off guard. My world spins faster, and I clutch the tree for support, nails digging into the coarse bark. My gaze shifts downward. Three of the beasts hold bows, arrows nocked into place.

Two more shoot past me, lodging into the wood beside my head.

Anger overcomes my nausea, and I shrug my bow free. I refuse to be beaten so easily, refuse to let them taunt me whilst I sit upon a branch, bleeding out so helplessly. I refuse to die so shamefully, so willingly.

I release an arrow into the night-ridden woods, pain lancing through my wound as I watch it strike a racai, giving it no time to react. It drops without a sound. My forearm throbs in response, and I am painfully aware of how much blood I have lost.

I prepare another arrow, easily deflecting the return fire.

Before they can nock another arrow, I fire two rounds.

Both beasts drop dead, and a fit of howls explodes beneath me.

I have only angered them further.

In a bout of rage, they begin to hurl their weapons at me, yet at such an angle, their throws are sloppy, misguided, and it takes little effort to deflect them. Their swords drop back onto the forest floor, futile.

I peer over, a tight smile curving my lips.

Eight remain.

I can do nothing more, not in my current state.

I sink down upon the branch, bow slung over my shoulder.

My eyes flutter, threatening to close and lull me into a blissful sleep, one I fear I shall not wake from. My fingers curl around the rough branch, both for support and something to ground me against the dizziness. The loss of blood has brought upon me a new, unrelenting wave of exhaustion, yet I cannot allow myself to give in to it, cannot let my guard slip. Glancing down at the racai, I notice them deep in conversation, voices too harsh and low to comprehend.

I cannot remain here. If I let my condition worsen, I will not survive much longer.

A thought strikes me.

With a grunt, I glance down at the beasts once more.

Now, only three remain. They pace beneath the tree, occasionally growling, their faces twisted into chilling sneers. The rest of the pack has left, departed towards the cave, leaving their companions to watch over me and warn them should I make any attempt to escape. Until then, they shall await in the safety of their hollow and shall only venture out should I attempt to escape, die on the spot, or tumble from the tree. Although the latter is preferable, for they shall wish to kill me themselves.

The beasts believe it to be some sort of twisted sport, where they torture their victims before — with the loss of their enjoyment — killing them. Yet now, their leave has granted me a reprieve—a chance to escape their horrid games.

Pressing myself into the trunk, I push onto my feet, hard bark scraping along my back. My eyes scan the darkness for any sign of Elwis, yet she is free from my sight. I bring my fingers to my lips, whistling.

Below me, the racai snarl, yet they cannot touch me up here.

My chest heaves with an unsteady breath, and I force myself to keep my eyes open. Bow cast over my shoulder, I yank a dagger free from my scabbard, using it to tear a piece of fabric from my forearm, leaving the gash exposed. I place the makeshift bandage over my wound, winding it about my arm before tying it tight enough to stem the flow of blood.

Yet it soaks through the fabric, staining it with the crystal-red of elven blood.

I have no choice but to let it bleed.

A sharp growl erupts from below me, followed by the thundering of hooves. I grasp the trunk, nails digging into the wood to support me as I peer over the edge. Elwis stands in the centre of the triangle of racai, her hooves moving rapidly through the air as she rears up, trying desperately to fend them off. The beast's weapons are brandished, and they spin the blades about their hands, snarling threateningly.

I act without a thought, afraid that if I think too long, I shall become too weak, too afraid to free myself from these creatures.

I leap from the tree, dropping into a summersault before landing in a crouched position behind one of the beasts. It spins to face me, dagger raised, and I roll beneath it, thrusting my blade back to clip its legs. The beast cries out, and I slam my dagger through its back, drawing my second blade.

The remaining racai circle me.

I do not have long before the rest of their horde returns, for the chaos shall have drawn their attention. Should they return before I can escape, I shall not survive, for I will be too weak to fight such a large number alone.

I strike before the beast does, thrusting my dagger towards its unprotected chest. It dodges me, swiping for my leg, yet I rotate out of the way, lodging my blade deep into its side. It drops to the ground, dead. Behind me, the last racai advances. I turn to meet it, capturing its sword between my blades. I twist them, jerking the weapon from its hands. Forcing both daggers through its stomach, I kick the beast to the ground, withdrawing my bloodied blades.

I tip my head back, breathless. A thin sheen of sweat coats my forehead, and as the adrenaline begins to wear off, the nausea and dizziness comes rushing back, crashing over me in a relentless wave. I stagger to Elwis's side, my vision swimming. Struggling to slide my daggers back into their sheaths, I fumble multiple times before succeeding and reaching for the pommel of my saddle. Lacking strength, I grapple with hoisting myself onto her back, and after a few attempts, I rest my forehead against the cool leather of my saddle, breathing deeply. Stars blot my vision, and my legs begin to tremble, threatening to give out.

I swallow hard, fingers tightening around the pommel in a wave of desperation and determination. With a burst of strength, I heave myself into the saddle. Dizziness overwhelms me, and I tilt to the side. Elwis whinnies, and I catch myself before I can fall. Gathering the reins in my hands, I clench them in my fists, tight enough for my knuckles to grow a ghostly white in seconds.

Elwis angles her head to the side, looking back at me. Her eyes are wide, fearful. She shakes her head, whinnying. I bend over, reaching down to pat her neck.

"Shh," I muse.

She snorts, pawing the ground in disapproval. I raise my head, looking through the break of trees ahead, my vision unfocused and my senses muted.

Shouts echo through the valley, laced with a promise of violence, and

I blink to clear my vision. Blurry figures emerge from the hollow, their voices rising, their frames growing as they become closer. Fear knotting in my throat, I kick Elwis's sides, urging her into a gallop. She bursts through the tree line, her hooves clicking upon the pebbles that line the shore, mingling with the zip of arrows — which narrowly miss my sides — and the beast's enraged shouts. I grip the pommel tightly, trying to keep myself from slipping into unconsciousness, from sinking so far into this blissful dark that I do not return.

When the racai's calls have faded, and I am free from their sights, the cave far behind, I look down at my wound, where blood has soaked through the fabric, leaking onto my exposed flesh, staining it red. It throbs in an excruciating rhythm, and I clench my jaw against the pain.

The gash is deep. Deeper than what I may be able to recover from.

# FIFTEEN
## THALIA

he next morning, I am awake at dawn.

I have slept longer than I intended, yet I care not. I have not slept in a real bed for many days and dared not to waste the opportunity to catch up on the much-needed energy which shall aid me in the days to come. It also granted me the opportunity to heal, to ease the soreness from my body, however little. Yet the pounding in my head remains, a faint yet persistent hammering at the back of my skull.

I push it to the back of my mind as I stand before the mirror once more, fully outfitted in my attire. My bracers are strapped on, my bow and quiver cast over my shoulder, daggers within their sheaths. My hair is pulled into its usual coiffure, a simple half up half down do, with two sections drawn to the back and braided down. I meet my own eyes in the mirror, searching their youthful emerald.

I drop my head, staring down at the dusty wooden boards. A cockroach scuttles across them, disappearing into a crevice. I inhale deeply, holding it for a moment, and my eyes fall closed. When I release my breath, I open them again, staring back into the mirror to steel myself for the days ahead. Straightening my posture, I hold my chin high. I will not let them see my pain. I will not let them see the sorrow in my eyes.

I will not let Killian hurt my heart as such, for I am tired of being so weak and dwelling on the past.

Turning, I stride to the door and into the dank hallway. I follow it to the right, then down the crooked stairs. I toss the keys onto the table without a word. The woman is asleep, her head dropped against the wooden desk, and her hair splayed messily about her.

I stride into the bar, where few people remain. Many are unconscious, their heads on the tables, with drinks spilt around them. Their snores echo through the space, and I wrinkle my nose at the scent of spiced wine and fresh vomit.

Quickly, quietly, I slip between the overturned tables and broken chairs into the foyer. The handle of the door is coarse beneath my fingertips, I turn it gently, and it shakes within its hold.

I step outside. The air is crisp, yet there is a warmth about it as if it is hinting at the day's coming heat. Moving out of the path, I lean against the wall, settling my hands on the hilt of my dagger. My eyes rove the street before me, the quiet alleys and cracked cobblestones. There is no movement. Nobody wandering this part of the village.

The door opens behind me, and I cock my head to the side, peering into the doorway. Ofen steps out. He is clad in an immaculate gold pauldron, yet not nearly as extravagant as Killian's silver, dragon-scale one. A sword is sheathed at his hip, a curved bow upon his back accompanied by a quiver embellished with gold.

"Took you long enough," I utter, an echo of his words.

Ofen swivels towards me, caught off guard by my presence. When he realises it is me, his lips curve into a grin.

"Forgive me, Your Majesty," he says, dropping into an exaggerated bow. I roll my eyes, pushing myself away from the wall.

"I must head to the market before we depart, for I need a map. You may accompany me if you so choose," I offer.

He bows his head. "I shall."

He begins to walk, and I fall into step beside him, following the quiet street towards the centre of the village, where the market is held.

"Sleep well?" I ask.

He shrugs, and for a moment, he is silent, staring down the cobblestone street, a weight beneath his stare. When his eyes return to me, he speaks, yet all traces of humour have vanished. "I had a few things on my mind."

I hold his gaze. He wants me to explain, to apologise for last night. He wants me to feel guilty.

"Yes, after our conversation, I suppose you would. Yet surely you understand why I could not explain everything to you in such a public area?" I ask, my tone deceptively calm.

"Yes, Thalia. I understand. I just—" He pauses, searching for words.

"Wish you did not have to find out in such a way?" I finish.

He looks back to me. "Yes."

I nod subtly. "I know. I wish I did not have to tell you. I *wish* it did not happen." I swallow, lacing my fingers together before me.

He lifts his chin, yet I can see the grief in his eyes. "I cannot imagine it, Thalia. I cannot imagine being there, *seeing it*, as you did. *Especially* alone."

"I was not alone."

He angles his head to me, chin dipping. "No?"

"No." His eyes bore into mine, a silent question within them, and before I can think, I reply, "Killian was there, too."

"Ah," he says, nodding. Although Killian and Ofen grew up in separate kingdoms, they have met a couple of times before. On a few rare occasions, most often during revels, I would have both Killian and Ofen with me, for when I was young, it was not uncommon for Arendul to travel to Enia, sometimes at the same time as I. He would bring Killian, and we three children would play among the sunlit corridors of Enia's palace.

"And where is he now?" he asks.

At that, I am silent.

When the quiet stretches on for too long, he halts, and I am forced to follow suit.

"Thalia?"

I set my jaw, tilting my head so that I may meet his eyes.

"Where is Killian?"

Emotion rises in my throat, and I twine my fingers tighter until my knuckles turn white.

"He heads to Lsthrain."

He raises a delicate eyebrow. "And why is that?"

"*Must* you ask so many questions, Ofen?" I hiss.

His lips part, yet no words escape, for something catches his eye. A shadow flickers from the street to my left, and I whirl, a hand immediately on the hilt of my dagger.

Ofen grunts and my gaze flicks back to him. Fear wells in my chest at the sight of him wide-eyed and struggling to free himself from the suffocating grasp of the man who holds him, dragging him down the street. I move to free my dagger, closing the distance.

My dagger is ripped from my hand, and from behind, my wrist is grasped and jerked behind my back. I suck in a breath, attempting to free myself, yet one hand comes across my stomach, holding me so tight that I may not escape. When I try to call out to Ofen, I am silenced, a muscular forearm covering my mouth. I struggle against the brute that holds me, yet I am no match for his strength. He whisks my struggling form away, down the alley where they have taken Ofen, forcing me to walk before him despite my resistance.

We wind down a couple of alleyways which branch off from the first. When we round the last corner, my fear rises, churning in the pit of my stomach. It is dimly lit, the hangover roofs blocking out the sunlight. A gang of burly men stand within the alley. Ofen is on his knees, arms held behind his back.

He turns his head, eyes widening when he sees me.

"Thalia—"

His head is jerked backwards by the hand clamped forcefully in his hair, and Ofen's eyes slam shut, a hiss passing between his teeth.

*"Silence."*

I writhe in the man's arms, trying to break free of his grasp, which only tightens. He slams me against the wall, face first, and I feel the rough surface scrape my cheek. A gasp passes my lips, the breath leaving my body. Grasping my long hair, he jerks me back, letting go so I stumble backwards, tripping on the uneven ground. I land beside Ofen, the coarse stone slicing my palms.

I reach for my dagger, but my hands are pulled behind my back before I may grip it. My weapons are removed alongside the blade he had taken earlier and then cast across the cobblestones.

"Who are you?" I demand.

Silence greets my question.

*"Who. Are. You?"*

I cry out as my hair is yanked once more, and I bite my lip to suppress a whimper. My scalp is burning, and my head is held back at an excruciating angle.

"You do not remember me?"

My body tenses at the voice.

"We met last night. Tell me you recall our encounter?"

My eyes dart to the man emerging from the shadows. He is menacingly tall, with a broad chest and shoulders. The same familiar, dangerous brown eyes stare back at me from the other end of the alley. I feel my anxiety spike.

"I cannot seem to recall last night. I must have been too inebriated," I lie, my voice laced with sarcasm. It is a cover for my unease, a show to prove I do not fear him.

He nods once, expressionless, as he crosses his arms over his vast chest.

I know I should stay silent, I know I should not provoke him, yet I cannot help myself. "Funny that you should care about the events of last night. One would have thought you could not stoop so low as to follow through on your threat of revenge. Surely one so bold has better things to do?"

He stiffens, muscles straining against his tight shirt.

"Brave, aren't ya?" He steps closer, leaning down before me. His eyes flicker with barely contained rage, and I lift my eyebrows in response.

"I recall you telling me the opposite when I spilt your drink."

His eyes darken. "Maybe foolish is more accurate."

"I like to think of it as a bit of both," I growl.

The ghost of a smile tugs at his lips. When he straightens, his gaze shifts to Ofen.

"Who is this?" He asks his men.

"He was with her," one of them replies.

"Mhm."

He continues to stare at Ofen, his eyes narrowed, and I fear what he may do to him, so I cut in, drawing his attention back to me.

"What do you want with us?"

The man tilts his head. "Do you not recall my words?"

I raise my eyebrows, a show of confidence. "Funny, they were not significant enough to stick in my mind."

In one swift movement, his fingers are closed around my throat, and I am slammed against the wall, the air knocked from my lungs. His elbow presses into my throat whilst the other hand moves to grip my jaw with crushing strength. I suck in a breath, yet the arm at my throat prevents air from entering my lungs. A strangled gasp escapes my lips, and I lift my chin in his grasp, my jaw set with defiance. He towers over me; his neck craned so that his eyes are trained upon mine.

From the corner of my eye, I see Ofen struggle against the men that hold him, a furious snarl escaping his lips. Yet his persistence earns him nothing but a fist to the jaw. I flinch at the sharp crack and the blood that coats the man's knuckles. Ofen sinks back onto the ground, no longer struggling.

"Being so reckless as to stumble into my table and spill *all* the drinks is one thing, but *threatening me?* That is something I do not take lightly, and I like to make my point clear. I like to make sure those who cross me regret doing so." He cocks his head in an act of intimidation. "And to make sure those mistakes are not repeated."

His reason is foolish; a spilt drink is no reason to seek somebody out. I believe he merely craves a fight. Gritting my teeth, I lean forward so my face is mere inches from his. "And I ask you once more, *will I regret it?*"

For a moment, the pressure upon my throat is relinquished, and I inhale sharply, my neck aching from the brute's strength. Yet my relief is short-lived, for the next moment, it is not his elbow against my throat but his dagger.

The blade nicks my throat, sharp and stinging, yet it is nothing to what I have endured. Not these recent days. Not in my lifetime.

I angle my head to the side, and the blade follows. "Do you know how many people have threatened me? Do you know how many blades I have had held to my throat?"

The blade drives closer to my skin, digging into my flesh.

*"Sindir was killed."*

*"Where is your evidence?"*

*Furious once again, he presses the dagger against my throat. I grit my teeth at the sting but refuse to yield.*

*"They seek revenge for their fallen ruler." There is something in his eyes, the same disquiet that had lingered there earlier, if only for a brief moment.*

*His ignorance heightens my anger.*

*"The racai spoke of something far from just revenge for their fallen ruler. You believe they alone would have the power to do as they did before without somebody to guide them? They cannot bring war upon us alone. It is not revenge they seek; it is something far more dangerous," I chide.*

*"I refuse to believe Sindir is alive."*

*"Then you are a fool."*

*He drives the dagger harder against my neck, and a sharp pain echoes in response. I tense, watching as his eyes break away from mine, drifting slowly to my throat, where I feel the warm trickle of blood.*

I lift my chin higher, trying to escape the tip of his dagger, and I feel myself tremble. Yet it is not fear but raw fury. All those emotions, all the anger and hurt and grief, come back to me, crashing over me in a suffocating wave. All the pain I have kept hidden for fear that it would swallow me whole. All the pain I have suppressed for fear of making myself appear vulnerable, weak.

"I have escaped *every. Single. Blade.*" I lean closer; my teeth barred, my words quiet and dangerous, laced with venom, laced with all the emotion I have kept pent up. "And yours shall be no different."

I hook my leg around the man's, swiping them out from beneath him. His knees buckle, and I twist the knife from his grip, catching him before he can hit the ground. I ball his shirt in my fist, spinning him around, then slamming him against the wall. I place the dagger below his collarbone, allowing the blade to press against his flesh just enough for him to feel the bite.

Behind me, there is scuffling, raised voices, and the unsheathing of blades. My fingers tighten about the hilt, and I dig the edge of the blade into his skin, drawing blood. It seeps into his white shirt, spreading slowly to stain it with a deep red.

"*Drop your weapons.*"

Silence.

I glance over my shoulder, careful not to relinquish my hold on the brute. They do not obey. Seething, I slam my elbow into the man's jugular.

Behind me, the blades clatter onto the cobblestones.

"Let go of my friend," I order.

When the men hesitate once more, anger rolls through me, and I lose control.

I slam the tip of the dagger into the brute's shoulder. His body stiffens, a darkness in his eyes as I hold his gaze, yet he does not fight me, for each time he tries to escape my grasp, I sink the blade deeper into his flesh. A pained growl passes his lips.

*"How about now?"*

Without hesitation, the men scramble, barking orders at one another. They release Ofen, and he brings himself to stand, grabbing one of the discarded weapons. He kicks the rest of them away, out of the gang's reach.

I turn back to the man. His jaw is clenched and a vein throbs in his neck. Pain is etched into his dark features.

"Not so brave now, are you?"

He is silent, those dangerous eyes flickering with rage.

"I am going to release you, and when I do, I want your word that you shall not pursue us."

His body grows rigid, jaw clenching tighter, yet he remains silent. In response, my grip on the dagger tightens, the blade still lodged into his shoulder. Blinded by rage, I twist the weapon, deepening the wound. His reaction is automatic, wincing as he tries to free himself from my grasp. I refuse to release him.

*"Do. I. Have. Your. Word?"*

He nods once, jaw tight, fists clenched.

I tilt my head smugly, my lips curving into a delicate smirk. "Good."

Without warning, I yank the dagger free, kicking it across the alley. I drop into a crouch, ducking beneath a lopsided punch. Reaching up, I grasp my assailants — a gang members — wrist, twisting it before sprinting to my weapons. I slide to the ground, reaching for my bow and quiver. Ofen steps before me, shielding me as I shrug them over my shoulder, now regaining my daggers. I keep them tight in my grasp as I stand, brandishing my blades before me.

I step out from behind Ofen, backing slowly down the alley. The gang has gathered in the centre, struggling to help their injured leader.

"I recommend you keep to your promise, for if you decide to come for us once more, I shall not be so merciful."

The brute's lips curve into a sneer, and I meet it with my own wicked smile.

Ofen and I round the corner, and as soon as we are out of sight, we break into a run, only slowing when we depart the eerie side street, where we are in a clear view of the village, where the men would not dare hurt us. Ofen grabs my arm, spinning me to face him. He has retrieved his weapons, and his sword is sheathed at his hip.

"Are you hurt?" He asks, panic lacing his words.

I stare at him.

Am I hurt?

Yes, yes, I am.

Physically? Barely. Yet I can feel the trickle of blood on my throat, feel the burn of my scalp where my hair was pulled. Yet, for the most part, I am unscathed.

Emotionally?

I no longer know how to answer such a question.

"I am fine," I reply. My gaze shifts to his jaw, to the blood staining his tanned skin. "*You* are not."

He reaches a hand up, brushing it over his injury. His features curve into a wince, and he lets his hand drop back to his side, to the hilt of his sword. "I will treat it, although it is nothing of major concern."

"Lies."

He raises an eyebrow, and I turn away from him, starting down the street, towards the market.

"Thalia?"

I tilt my head, meeting his eyes through a curtain of hair.

"I ask of you one thing."

I do not respond, fearing his question.

"I know you are battling with something, something you refuse to speak of, and I respect that. I cannot, *will not* force you to speak to me of your struggles, yet I ask of you one thing. I must know what happened in Enia. That is something I deserve to be told."

Averting my gaze, I twine my fingers before me, daggers back in their sheaths. Ofen is correct, I cannot deny him this truth, nor do I have any desire to.

I only fear his reaction.

Fear he shall blame me for the kingdom's downfall, for Calivar's death, just as I blame myself.

I bow my head. "Yes, you do."

We continue in silence for a few moments until Ofen grasps my hand, and I halt, turning to face him. He drops my hand, instead laying his own on my shoulder. His eyes search mine.

"I am not asking you to trust me, Thalia, but I wish you to know that you can talk to me," he pauses. "You can talk to me about whatever you are going through, about your struggles. *Anything*."

I chew on the inside of my cheek, unsure of how to respond or put my thoughts into words. "I do trust you, Ofen. I *want* to talk; I *want* to share my feelings. I am just—"

"Afraid?"

I grow silent, searching his face. "That is it, Ofen. I am tired of being afraid, afraid of being vulnerable and weak. And I am *tired* of being hurt. Of having my heart broken. Of losing *everyone* and *everything* I care about." I swallow, limbs trembling with emotion. "So yes, I suppose in a way it is about trust, but more so, it is about losing myself. Because with everything, *everyone* I lose, I feel as though I lose a piece of my heart. A piece of *myself*, and I am tired of having to build myself back up."

I step away from him, and his hand drops back to his side. We are both silent, trying to decipher the thoughts hidden beneath each other's expressions. When I can no longer take the silence, I say: "I cannot waste any more time, I have already lingered in this village too long. I need to find a map," — I look down at my tattered garments — "and new attire."

Without awaiting his response, I continue toward the market.

# SIXTEEN
## KILLIAN

he moment I know I am free of the beasts, I bring Elwis to the shoreline. My forearm is pulsing with pain, hanging limp at my side, knuckles still bloody. I cannot keep my eyes from fluttering, cannot keep the exhaustion at bay.

How tempting it is to give into the darkness, to sleep. Yet, in a state such as mine, I know that if I give in, I may never wake.

With trembling limbs, I dismount, staggering to the water's edge. I drop down onto the pebbles, wasting no time unwrapping my wound. My vision swirls, and I feel myself sway unsteadily despite my perched position on the shoreline. The gash is deep, swelling with warm, crystal-red blood. It is encircled by jagged teeth marks. I grit my teeth at the pain but cannot stop myself from crying out when I dip my arm into the river, allowing the calm water to flow over my flesh, tearing through the slit with a sharp sting. The pain is sudden and excruciating, and the nails of my opposite hand dig into my flesh to withstand the hurt, etching tiny crescents into my skin. When it has finally dulled to a throb, I am able to better clean the wound and then rewrap it in a fresh strip of fabric, now free from infection. Once done, I scrub my knuckles, ridding the blood from my skin to reveal multiple red cuts and bruises.

With a grunt, I shift onto my knees, the swirling of my thoughts and persistent dizziness finally easing. I cup my hands together before dipping them into the river, then splash the cool water upon my face, allowing it to heighten my awareness and dull my exhaustion.

I blink once, twice, clearing my blurred vision. The lightheadedness remains, as does the tiredness and unsteadiness. And although they are not as relentless as before, I am still weak. Too weak. My eyes are tired, flickering, and I cannot think straight.

Nevertheless, one thing is clear in my mind. If I am to remain here, in the open, there is no doubt the beasts shall find me again.

Before standing, I dip my hands into the water once more, taking a sip to quench my thirst. Then, I stumble to my feet, gripping Elwis's saddle to steady myself. For a moment, the world spins, and I am forced to close my eyes to slow the swimming. After a moment, I adjust my grip on the saddle, allowing my nails to dig into the leather as I hoist myself onto Elwis's back with a burst of strength.

As soon as I am settled in the seat, I grip the reins, muscles straining against my shirt as I hold them tight, fingers curled around the leather, knuckles white. I click my tongue, fighting my exhaustion as she begins across the shore, hooves tapping against the rocks. As we continue forward, towards the trail Thalia and I took through Enia's mountains, I force myself to keep my eyes open, despite their constant fluttering. I must find a place to rest, for I am too exposed by the river.

Amidst the silence, fatigue and pain, my mind threatens to return to Thalia.

And how badly I wish she were here.

# SEVENTEEN
## THALIA

he streets are lined with vendors and carts, some with fresh fruits and vegetables and meats, others with clothes and trinkets, although they sell the same items for the most part. It is only a matter of where the best price can be found.

Ofen and I have equipped ourselves with a healthy amount of food, enough to suffice for the next few days of our travels and ration should it come to it. And, with the worn state of my garments, I managed to get my hands on a cheap set of attire. It is simple, with black trousers and a tight sort of cloak, reaching mid-thigh and split down the middle to reveal the black shirt I now wear beneath. A gold string stretches around my waist, cinching it.

"Oh, there," I say, tilting my head toward the table to our right. Ofen follows me to the table, where an arrangement of maps has been rolled up and tied with fraying ribbons. I pick one up, carefully untying the string to unroll the map.

The paper is snatched from my hands, and I startle, my gaze darting to the woman before me. She leans over the table, her piercing eyes locked on mine, the map crushed beneath her bony fingers.

117

"Don't touch unless yer buying it."

I raise my eyebrows, allowing my gaze to do a quick sweep over her, her curly and untamed grey and white hair, the tattered clothes that hang off her skeletal figure.

"Who says I am not?"

She narrows her eyes, straightening her spine — as much as her hunched back shall allow — and staring at me for a few moments, her prickly eyes giving me a slow once over. I tilt my head in response, a silent challenge as I motion to the maps laid out on the table. "How much?"

Her cracked lips tip up in response.

"Five gold ethereals."

I recoil in shock and disgust, my eyes widening dramatically. Beside me, I hear Ofen scoff.

"*Five?* Do you have any idea how much a single of those coins is worth?" He snaps.

The woman smiles giddily at Ofen, her eyes wide. "I've named me price."

He tips his head back in frustration, then locks his fingers around my wrist, gently guiding me away from the table and back down the street. When I resist, he spins to face me.

"I need a map, Ofen."

He releases a breath. "We shall find one elsewhere, Thalia."

"And you think they shall be any less expensive?"

He does not respond.

"Ofen, we do not easily blend into this crowd. They know we are not from around these parts." I gesture towards our pointed ears. "Their prices shall be raised for us wherever we go, so we might as well not waste our time searching for another seller."

He releases my arm, touching his tongue to the inside of his cheek as he contemplates. Finally, he shakes his head once. "All right, Thalia. But do not do anything you shall regret."

My lips tip up in a mischievous grin.

"Me? Never."

He chuckles quietly, shaking his head at my response as I turn away, returning to the vendor, where I slap one of Alistar's coins down on the table, leaning forward to brace my hands on its edge. The woman's eyes light up, her lips parting into a grin.

And then it slips away, twists into a sneer, and her eyes dart to mine.

"*Five.*"

"*One.* It is more than enough for what I shall receive in return and shall cover your meals for two weeks, at the least."

A growl rises in her throat.

"No."

"Would you rather I find somewhere else to spend my coin?" A lie, but one I hope she cannot see through.

She throws her head back, cackling. "Ungrateful woman. You stand no chance against those other business folks. What I'm giving ya is a steal."

*A steal.*

"Mhm." I tilt my head, casting a glance over my shoulder to make sure Ofen is near. He stands in the same spot I had left him, our recently bought goods held in a small satchel cast over his shoulder. His eyes meet mine, and I turn back to the woman, straightening my spine.

"One or nothing, you can take it, or you can leave it. Your choice."

Her eyes flicker between me and the coin, an indecisiveness in her expression. Finally, she hardens her gaze and speaks with a firm "No."

I shrug carelessly. "Pity."

And then I snatch a map from the table and run.

Her scream erupts into the air, high-pitched and witch-like, and I wonder for a moment if I have made a mistake, yet it is far too late for that now, for the attention of those around us has been caught by her screech, and every pair of eyes is on me.

A spark shoots up my spine, and I bite my lip against the smile curling my lips at the thrill. I do not know what has possessed me, but despite the fear, there is a rush of adrenaline, and as I run past a shocked Ofen, grasping his arm to drag him along with me, a laugh escapes me.

"Thalia, what—"

Perhaps it is the change of pace from the guilt, regret, and sadness that had clouded my mind since the day Killian left. Perhaps it is the sudden rush of adrenaline getting to me, but I cannot ignore the thrill of racing down the streets, dodging civilians as we sprint towards the inn. Angered shouts rise behind us, and I hear the familiar clink of armour, the brush of steel against scabbard as a blade is drawn. Guards.

"Thalia!"

Ofen's voice reaches me, and I spin to face him, stumbling as I come to an abrupt halt. He stands at the entrance to an alleyway, motioning frantically for me to follow. I shoot a glance into the crowds, where I can see the guards approaching, shoving people out of their way, and I sprint after Ofen, following him into the shadowed side street.

Crates line the walls of the buildings that close us in, and Ofen directs me as we run side by side, the sentries' calls echoing after us. My heart beats frantically within my chest, which heaves with exertion.

A stray cat darts from the shadows and into my path, and a surprised yelp escapes my lips as I swerve to avoid it, staggering into a pile of boxes, tipping them over with a loud crash. I wince, finding Ofen's widened eyes.

His lips part, but the shouts of the guards cut him off, much closer than before, and we take off once more, winding through the narrow and curvy alleyways until we reach the one behind The Filly.

Alwyne whinnies in greeting and I skid to a stop before him. Ofen halts momentarily at my side, chest heaving with each ragged breath. He places a gentle hand between my shoulder blades. "Meet me at the stables."

I bow my head, and he is gone, disappearing around the bend and into view of passersby.

I fumble with the buckle of my satchel as the footfalls of the guards grow closer, and a panicked sound escapes my throat as I shove the map inside, frantically clipping the buckle and slicing through Alwyne's binds with my dagger. I hoist myself into the saddle as the sentries appear at the end of the alleyway, shouting and pointing at me.

I kick his sides, grasping the reins as I turn him away, clicking my tongue as Alwyne takes off, charging into the street, his hooves clicking against the cobblestone.

"Ofen!" I scream his name as we near the barn, the sentries close now. Too close.

Panic rises, making my stomach flop back and forth. I round the barn, halting outside the side doors. I shout his name again, and not moments later, Ofen bursts outside, swinging himself into the saddle.

"Follow my lead!" He shouts over the rising chaos.

Pressing his leg into his horse's side, he turns, placing his back to both myself and the guards before taking off down the side street towards the edge of the caged-in village. Alwyne needs no command in following Ofen's departure.

The cobblestone clicks beneath Alwyne's hooves as we race after Ofen through the alleyways and low-hanging roofs, chased by the shouts of the guards, which are echoed by our own reckless apologies to those we narrowly miss hitting.

Heavy footfalls ricochet off the walls around me, and I tilt my head, catching sight of those who pursue us, now upon horses of their own.

*Damn it.*

I turn back to Ofen, a gasp catching in my throat when I am almost decapitated by a drooping clothing line. Instead, the clothes smack against my face, and I shove them out of my way, blinking rapidly as Alwyne continues after Ofen.

Behind, the sentries do not let up.

I touch my tongue to the inside of my cheek in frustration, then reluctantly slip my bow into my hand, reaching back for an arrow. Their calls rise in volume, desperation lacing their words. A small smirk curves my lips. I release the reins, allowing them to rest against Alwyne's neck as I nock the dragon-tip arrow into place and draw the string against my cheek. Ahead, there is a rickety wooden cart. Few rotting apples are set within, flies buzzing about them as they anxiously await their latest meal. Beneath the wheels are tiny pebbles, unsteady in their attempt to keep the cart in place.

The slightest jolt and it is gone.

I squint against the glare of sunlight, and then my fingers are gliding along the string, my arrow slicing diagonally through the air. The pebble skitters across the cobblestones and bounces off the wall, knocked free of its holster by my arrow.

And then the cart begins to roll.

Screams erupt in response to my arrow and the runaway cart, and I meet Ofen's eyes as he looks back at me, a mischievous glint within them.

Alwyne whinnies, panicked as the cart speeds towards us.

It misses us by a hair, and the bounce of the wheels against the stone is met by the flurry of shouts rising from the guards. There is a loud crash and the whinny of frenzied horses. I chance a glance behind me. The cart has crashed into the wall, breaking off loose boards and tipping it over. Rotten apples roll through the streets, and the horses frantically back up, rearing and whinnying, the cart blocking their path.

A grin lifts my lips as I turn, hauling my bow back over my shoulder and once again taking the reins as Alwyne navigates the streets. Eventually, we come to the edge of the village. Ofen slows to a walk, glancing behind me before leading his horse around the back of the row of buildings. He slides out of the saddle, bunching the reins upon his horse's neck before treading to the end of the alley, where planks lean against the stone wall that surrounds the kingdom, the wood punctured where rats last feasted.

I cock my head to the side, watching with curiosity as he pulls the planks aside, dropping them to the cobblestone with a smooth crack.

There is a jagged hole in the wall.

My brows raise as Ofen turns back to me, and I nod to the hole. "How did you know this was here?"

The corner of his lips lifts into a lopsided smile. "You gain knowledge of the places you frequent, Thalia."

"And you frequent Verila?"

He brings the reins over his horse's head, leading it to the wall. "I travel often, and it is usually an easy place to reside for a night."

I scoff. "Easy."

His lips tug up. "Usually in the path of my travels. Although, after this visit, I doubt coming back shall be wise."

"Mhm," I reply, a smile tracing my lips.

I slip off Alwyne's back, drawing the reins over his head before halting behind Ofen.

"Watch your head."

I wait for him to walk through, ducking low to keep from bumping his head against the jagged arch of the hole. Then, I follow behind him, watching my footing across the littering of sharp-edged stones. He leaves his horse by the wall before slipping back through the crack to replace the planks, leaving no trace of our being here.

"Well, was that not fun?"

I tip my head back with a laugh, and the sun warms my face, making my smile linger for a few moments. When I drop my gaze back to Ofen's, he is grinning.

"So, you journey to Thilia?" I ask.

He bows his head. "Indeed."

"Intriguing," I reply, pulling the map from my satchel and spreading it across Alwyne's saddle.

Ofen's chuckle reaches my ears as he comes to my side. "The king is an old friend of mine."

My lips tip up.

At the edge of the map rests Lsthrain, Orathin on the opposite side, and diagonal from it is Verila. Below Lshtrain is Thilia, the two kingdoms separated by a mountain range and the Forest of Undying Souls. It is a kingdom of dwarves who dwell in and beneath the mountains, although I have never ventured there.

"Our paths allow us to journey together, if only for a short time," I pause, hesitating. "I shall explain everything to you on the way."

I roll up the map, slipping it into my satchel as I haul myself onto Alwyne's back.

"Thalia."

Gathering the reins, I tip my head down to meet Ofen's eyes. He stands beside his horse, a pouch in his hands. With a lopsided smile, he tosses me the bag. It is full of the food we gathered from the market earlier, a rationing of bread, cheese and berries. Enough for our journeys if we ration, extra should something not go to plan, so long as we are careful with our consumption.

I dip my head with a faint smile, then click my tongue, urging Alwyne into a trot. We take off, Ofen quickly gaining on us and falling into a steady rhythm at my side as we ride through the fields encircling Verila. We head further from The Burial Grounds, from Endalin and the others.

From Killian.

Once we have put a distance between the village and ourselves, I bring Alwyne to a walk, not wishing to drain his energy. The silence allows my mind to wander, an earlier memory freeing itself from the back of my mind. My gaze wanders the field, tracking the short, dull green grass. Much duller than the rich vibrancy of the field below Enia's mountains, where Killian and I rode after our departure from Lsthrain. Here, it is bare, an expanse of muted green scattered with nothing more than a few bare dandelions swaying gently in the crisp breeze.

"Thalia?"

Ofen's voice breaks the silence, and I turn my gaze to him. He watches me silently, patiently, and I know what he expects of me.

"There is a lot to explain, Ofen."

His eyes track mine for a moment. "I can only imagine."

Knowing I cannot evade his questions any longer, I start from the beginning, explaining everything from the troll scout to the Blood Riders. I stop before explaining Enia, choosing my words carefully, unsure how to relay what happened.

"During our trek through the mountains, we crossed paths with the beasts, both Blood Riders and Racai. They travelled the trail below us, although after the rockslide we caused, I thought we killed them all—"

"You caused a *rockslide?*"

My gaze dips to Ofen, to his widened eyes and parted lips. Disbelief is written upon his features, and I feel my lips twitch at the memory. "Indeed."

His lips tug into a small smile.

"After we arrived in Enia, I awoke during the night. There was a noise from the corridor, something I could not discern, and Killian burst in. He tried to explain the situation. He led me to the window—" I pause for fear my voice shall break, and take a shuddering breath to keep it steady, to keep the emotion at bay. "The city was on fire, Ofen."

The silence stretches, and I allow it to, giving Ofen time to process my words. After a short time, I speak once more.

"There was nothing I could do— I wanted to stay, I wanted to fight alongside Calivar and his kingdom, but—" I swallow my tears. "There was nothing I could do; nothing *we* could do. The kingdom was already beyond repair. The bridges were on fire, and the homes— Killian and I barely made it out alive."

When I turn my gaze to Ofen, he is staring ahead, his jaw set, the sorrow in his eyes clouded by a swirling, consuming darkness.

Although I fear his answer, I force the words out. "Do you blame me, Ofen?"

He turns to me, eyebrows knitted, lips parted. There is a hint of hesitation as he stares at a point beyond my shoulder; the grief now conquered the darkness.

"No, Thalia, of course I do not. Why would I blame you?"

"Because even I blame myself, Ofen."

His head drops against his chest. "I can understand why you may feel such a way, Thalia. I would feel the same had it been me, but you could not have stopped them. Enia is a powerful kingdom, but it is not unbreakable. You could not have known they would come."

But could I?

Killian and I spotted them on the mountain trail. We created the rockslide to kill them. We *thought* we killed them all.

But what if we did not? What if there were more of them? What if they followed us to Enia?

I wrap the reins about my index finger, trying to take my mind away from the thought.

We ride in silence for a while, and now and then, I chance a glance at Ofen, yet he never meets my gaze. He is too lost in his thoughts, his eyes clouded, his expression blank, distant as he stares ahead. In the silence, it is hard to keep my thoughts at bay, so I focus on the field, on the dandelions and their faded yellow, on the grass, and on the way their stems are jumbled together.

"What came after?"

Ofen is looking at me now, his eyes searching mine as he awaits my response.

"We travelled to Endalin. Calivar mentioned a favour the king owed him, hoping it would be of use to us. From there, we were accompanied by a few of the king's men and his daughter—"

"His daughter?"

I bow my head. "Yes. Although it was not of the king's choice, I suspect he has men searching for her. She came of her own accord."

He raises an eyebrow. "Sounds rebellious."

"It was."

"I suppose you two made good friends, then?"

To my surprise, I laugh. "When we were not fighting for our lives, yes."

His smile fades, and I continue. "We made our way to the Burial Grounds. That was where we found Valindor. Killian and I were separated from the others in the tunnels, and when we emerged, Killian's father was there, accompanied by his men. But then— then, we were ambushed by the racai." I nibble on my lip, reluctant. "I tried to save Valindor, to keep them from getting it, but I could not."

I shudder as I take a breath.

"That is why I travel to Orathin, to retrieve Valindor before the racai can pass it on to their leader, Sindir. Before it is too late."

"And you plan to do this alone? To travel to Orathin, to steal Valindor straight from the racai and their leader without their knowledge?"

I bow my head. "What choice do I have, Ofen?"

"A few."

I lower my eyes. "If only."

"Killian."

My hands clench tighter about the reins, knuckles turning a ghostly shade. "He travels to Lsthrain, Ofen, as I told you."

"Not of his own accord."

"*Yes*, Ofen. Of his own accord." The more he pushes the subject, the more resentful I become.

"Lies," he says, echoing my words.

"Ofen—"

"I do not know Killian well, yet I know from what I have heard of your friendship, from what I have seen of you together, from the way you would speak of one another, he would not leave of his own accord. Maybe in a moment of anger, but maybe more so because of *your* anger, Thalia. Have you considered he may have left *for* you, not *because* of you?"

At that, I am speechless. My lips part, yet the words die in my throat. Despite my reluctance to admit it, there may be some truth to Ofen's words. Killian and I have fought before, but never in such a way. We have always made up. Never have we held a grudge for this long. Killian only ever did what he believed was best, and in truth, I would have sacrificed Valindor for him, too.

What a fool I have become.

*Love makes fools of us all.*

"What you said earlier, Thalia. It was about Killian, was it not?"

*I am tired of being hurt. Of having my heart broken. Of losing everyone and everything I care about.*

Yes, I suppose it was.

My parents. Grimsmith. Calivar.

But Killian most of all.

I nod.

A few seconds pass before Ofen speaks. "You have not lost him, Thalia. Everybody must walk their own paths, although I have no doubt yours are intertwined. Sometimes, it takes losing something, or *somebody*, to realise just how much we truly need them."

I want to cry again.

I want to wallow in a puddle of my own self-pity.

I want to find Killian and apologise for everything, for what I said, for what I did. I do not want to lose him, to shatter our friendship of so many years. He does not deserve my anger, for all he has ever done is be there for me. Never once has he put me down or discouraged me.

Yet I do not have the courage to face him yet, and even if I had the option to, I cannot turn back. I came for Valindor, and so I shall retrieve it. I have no choice, no matter the weight of my guilt.

Killian does not deserve my anger.

And a part of me wonders if maybe I do not deserve him.

# EIGHTEEN
## KILLIAN

lwis continues alongside the river, occasionally shaking her head or whinnying to keep me from drifting into unconsciousness. I try to focus on my surroundings, on the gentle breeze rustling the leaves of the trees, on the click of pebbles beneath Elwis's hooves. Try to focus on the trickle of water at my side, at the moon's reflection, casting a shimmering glow upon the valley's river.

Yet nothing dulls the pain.

Nothing dulls the exhaustion nor the emptiness in my heart.

Eventually, a slope comes into view. It descends from the mountains surrounding what was once Enia, and curves downwards at a steep incline, arriving at the shore of the river.

A ball of emotion clogs my throat at the sight of it, at the memory that resurfaces—a memory of Thalia. Of the last time we travelled this valley. Travelled this slope.

I urge Elwis past it, where the pebbled ground narrows, leaving just enough room for us to continue around a bend, out of sight. There, I find a cave. It is cramped, yet shall be enough to house both Elwis and me for the night.

Gripping the saddle, I free my feet from the stirrups. Careful upon the narrow shoreline, I drop to the ground, holding tight to the leather seat as the world spins. I rest my forehead against the saddle, the smooth material cool against my skin.

For a moment, I just breathe.

I count my breaths and inhale, exhale.

My eyes flutter closed, my chest rising and falling slowly as I try to settle the whir of thoughts, the whir of emotions that I try so hard to vanquish. My forearms rest against the leather seat, and I find myself twining my fingers together, squeezing them together to expel this awful, empty feeling.

After a few minutes, I raise my head, searching the darkness that cloaks me. I remain alone.

Carefully, I sidestep around Elwis, gathering the reins into my hands; I draw them over her head, then step into the cave. I brush my hand beneath her mane, a gesture of appreciation. She snorts softly in response, her eyes sparkling. Although I wish I could remove her tack and allow her some freedom from the saddle upon her back, I cannot risk it, for if the racai are to find us, I shall need her to be ready for a quick escape.

The sun shall rise in a few mere hours, and until then, I must get what rest I can.

For at dawn, I ride to Lsthrain.

# NINETEEN
## THALIA

he sunlight glares down from the sky, highlighting the dull green grass and withering dandelions, which slowly begin to fade as we near the edge of the field. There, the grass dissolves into a copse of trees.

I tug lightly on the reins, waiting for Ofen to follow suit. He turns in his saddle, gripping the back of the seat as he raises his brows.

"This is no longer your path, Ofen."

His throat bobs. "I know."

I lift my brows in question, and he cocks his head with a sigh. "I shall accompany you to Orathin, Thalia, but from there, I can go no further. The border is my barricade, for I still must make it to Thilia in good time."

My chest grows heavy with emotion, with the weight of his words and his willingness to follow me into this territory.

A weak smile graces my lips as I stare up at him. "Thank you, Ofen. It means more than you know."

His lips quirk. "It is my pleasure, Thalia."

Clicking my tongue, I urge Alwyne to his side, where we continue our ride towards the forest ahead.

"I presume you have not been to Orathin before?"

Ofen looks to me. "No, I have not."

His answer does not surprise me, for who would travel there of their own accord?

"Why do you ask?"

"Because a map can only tell you so much of a place."

Without awaiting his response, I click my tongue, urging Alwyne into the woods. The sunlight is snatched away by a sudden, unexpected blanket of darkness, which blocks out the rays of warmth with its towering copse of trees. All colour has been drained from the forest, leaving a dull mixture of greys and browns, an unsettling sight.

This place is not much different from the undying forest.

The realisation forms a lump of dread in the pit of my stomach.

"This is not wise, Thalia."

Ofen appears at my side, and I tip my head to him, yet do not respond, for I am not prepared to argue over such a thing. There is no changing my mind. I have come this far and shall not let this slip away as I had Valindor. Not after everything and everyone I have sacrificed. Not for all that is at risk.

"Thalia."

I turn to him, letting my eyes bore into his. "I will not argue over this, Ofen. I appreciate you accompanying me more than you know, but I understand if you wish to turn back and continue to Thilia as you planned. You cannot change my decision."

For a moment, he is silent. "There must be another way, Thalia. You cannot face these beasts alone."

"If you have another idea, please share."

His gaze leaves mine, returning to the eerie forest ahead, where the trees are shrouded in a white mist.

"There must be others willing to join your cause, others who will journey to this place with you, retrieve Valindor at your side," he pauses. "Come to Thilia with me. I know the king quite well; I am sure I could persuade him to send a small army into the kingdom with you. I, too, will join."

I take a breath, chest heaving. "I do not have time for that, Ofen. By the time we reach Thilia, the racai will have already delivered Valindor into the hands of Sindir. It will be too late."

"Then we can—"

"Nothing, Ofen. We can do nothing. I came here knowing I would complete this quest alone, and so that is what I shall do."

His gaze drops to the ground, and he says nothing in response. Dead leaves crunch beneath the horse's hooves, breaking the silence that follows my statement. The sound is eerie against the otherwise silent forest.

"I will be fine," I say gently, prompting him to meet my eyes.

His mouth quirks into a slight smile. "I know you will, Thalia. You are stronger than any who I have met. I only wish you did not have to leave so soon. We have only just reunited, after all."

The thought makes my heart drop, and my mind returns to the reunion I had shared with Calivar.

Right before Enia fell.

I urge Alwyne closer to Ofen and reach out, placing my hand upon his shoulder. "I have fought many battles before, Ofen, and here I stand. We shall see each other soon, that I can promise."

He bows his head.

"I will hold you to it."

My lips curve into a smile. "I should hope so."

*

We continue our journey through the forest, traversing around the kingdom at a safe distance to ensure we are not seen. Beyond the forest's border, the trees fade into swamp. We halt only when the trees ahead break apart and a small rocky ledge is visible, hanging only a short distance higher than the swamplands. For a while, we stand side-by-side, silent as we stare at the scene before us. At the mist encasing the trees, pockets of the fog crackling with purple energy, much like that found upon the Blood Rider's horses. We study the cliff face, illuminated in the last rays of dying sunlight. Had I not known the realm before me, it would have been an eerie, picturesque scene.

On our way here, we had stopped momentarily at a small stream, filling our stomachs and gathering berries to fuel us through the last of our travels. Ofen had been able to clean the wounds inflicted upon him by our captors in the village. His jaw remains sore, but it is a minor bruising and shall soon heal.

"I shall wait until nightfall," I say.

I continue to survey the land before me, but after a few moments, I feel Ofen's gaze on me. I turn to meet his eyes.

"I shall wait till then," he says. "Then I must ride for Thilia."

I swallow the lump in my throat, an inkling of fear curling around my heart at the mention of his leave. "Thank you," I say, my voice a murmur. I bow my head, a gesture of my appreciation, which he returns.

We dismount, searching for a place to await the darkness, a place concealed from the view of Sindir's beasts.

Yet the longer I wait, the slower the shadows seem to fall, the faster my heart seems to beat, and the higher my anxiety seems to rise.

For when dusk arrives, I shall journey into Sindir's realm.

# TWENTY
## THALIA

y back is pressed against a downed log, the sharp bark digging through the fabric of my shirt and into my flesh. The forest is near silent; the only sound is the eerie call of ravens in the distance, their cries echoing in the quiet of this dreadful wood. In response, my stomach churns with anxiety, curdling with the food I consumed when we arrived in this retched place, and it brings with it a wave of nausea that has me grimacing.

Readjusting my position to ease the sickness, I grasp my daggers to keep them slipping from where they are strewn across my lap. I toy with one of the gold hilts, running my fingers over its cool surface and smooth engravings. It is a reminder of my home, of the darkness within Lsthrain, the cold stone walls and dark caverns, the lush greenery spread throughout. The elves that dwell there, their lips curved into smiles, laughing with one another. Of the celebrations held atop Lsthrain's core, revels beneath the moonlight. Of my quarters, although bare, dark, they were *mine*.

It. Was. *Home.*

Despite Arendul's distaste towards me, despite my place as a commoner, I cannot deny how much I love that kingdom, for it is the place that has shaped me and gifted me with so many things.

With the person I care about the most.

With my best friend.

With *Killian*.

"You should get some rest."

I lift my head, fingers stilling on the handle of my dagger. Ofen stands before me, hand resting on the hilt of the sword which rests at his hip.

"I shall wake you once darkness has fallen."

I hesitate, then, "I doubt I shall sleep." Despite my feigned smile and failed attempt at humour, it does not fool Ofen. He does not return my attempt at lightheartedness.

"Try," he says delicately.

I press my tongue to the inside of my cheek in indecision, running my hand carefully along the surface of my blade. "You shall wake me when night has fallen, when the darkness will be enough to shield me, and if you see anything, hear anything, you inform me, okay?"

His lips quirk into a smile. "As you wish, Milady."

I kick his leg lightly, but he dances out of my reach.

"Fool," I chide, yet cannot help the smile curling my lips.

"You will get used to it, just as you did when we were children."

I raise my eyebrows, tilting my head to meet his gaze as he takes a seat beside me, back against the log.

"If you say so, Ofen," I reply, and he chuckles quietly in response.

Slipping my daggers into their sheaths, I pull the edges of my cloak around myself, a protection against the bitter chill of this forest, of the evening air.

Then, allowing my eyes to close, I drift into a dreamless sleep.

*

Sometime during my slumber, I awaken. The forest is eerily quiet; there is nothing, not even the soft crackle of a fire. I shift, fingers curled stiffly about the edges of my cloak.

Exhaustion claws at me, begging me to fall back into the darkness, yet I pry my eyes open. They flutter, the world slowly coming into bleary focus. I lie on my side, my shoulder resting roughly against the log. Biting my lip, I readjust myself, my body aching from the uncomfortable position. But with the sudden exhaustion, the pain seems distant.

Before me, a figure shifts, sword slipping quietly from its scabbard. Ofen.

I take a steadying breath, trying to calm the unexpected rush of emotions boiling in my stomach.

Because however much I appreciate Ofen for being here with me, for allowing me to rest whilst he watches for danger, I cannot help wishing it was Killian at my side.

# TWENTY-ONE
## THALIA

"Thalia."

I startle, quickly rolling onto my back and propping myself onto my elbows, fingers curling around the hilt of my dagger as I move to free it. Ofen grasps my shoulders, and my heart pounds as he stills me. His face is foggy, the world behind him spinning in a blur of dark trees and white fog. I squeeze my eyes shut, trying to dispel the sensation, yet it only worsens, and I force myself to take slow, steadying breaths.

The effects of my head injury, which have not fully healed.

Swallowing, I open my eyes carefully, aware of Ofen watching me, concern clouding the flecks of gold in his hazel eyes. His hands tighten upon my shoulders, and I feel the world slowly come back into focus.

"What happened?"

Planting my hands in the dirt, I shift backwards, pressing my back against the log and breaking free of his hold.

"Nothing, it is but a mere injury."

His eyebrows crease. "Injury?"

I nod. "I acquired it during one of my recent battles when the racai stole Valindor." I meet his gaze. "I suppose it is the reason they gained

Valindor."

His gaze searches mine, his jaw set as he tries to decipher my words, yet I wave his distress away. "I am fine, Ofen. I have survived this long."

I haul myself onto my feet, biting my lip against the sudden wave of dizziness, yet remain determined to conceal it.

The last rays of sunlight have slipped away, leaving the forest in blackness, yet with my enhanced elven sight; I am able to navigate it, as is Ofen. The darkness here is different from that of the undying forest, for here, it seems that a dwindle of hope remains in the shadows. Here, it does not seem to swallow you whole, despite its place near Sindir's realm.

I can only pray it is not false hope.

I look ahead to where the trees part in the distance and reveal the jagged cliffside, which is cast in silver moonlight.

"I suppose this is where we part?"

Slowly, I draw my gaze back to Ofen. His eyes flit over mine, sadness softening the delicate lines of his face.

"Yes, I suppose it is," I reply quietly.

For a moment, we are both silent.

"Then I wish you well, Thalia."

"And I you."

He steps up to me, coiling his strong arms around me in a reassuring embrace.

"Remember our promise," he murmurs.

"Of course," I return, nodding. "Thank you, Ofen."

"It is my pleasure, Thalia. Anytime you need me, I am here," he replies.

Swallowing the lump in my throat, the fear clawing at my ribcage, we stand in silence for a few moments, reluctant to step away. When I finally step out of his embrace, his eyes linger on mine for a moment.

"I will see you again soon."

One corner of his mouth tugs into a gentle smile. "And Valindor will be in your possession once more."

"Yes," I swallow my doubt. "It will."

Then, Alwyne at my side, I make for the forest's border.

*

I halt a few paces from the tree line, carefully tucking Alwyne into a nestle of shadows, where he is concealed from the beast's prying eyes. My fingers trip over his soft coat, his warmth a reassurance.

"I shall not be long," I muster, yet it is more for myself than Alwyne. Resting my forehead against his, I try to calm the dread coursing through my veins. When I pull away, there is a glimmer in his dark eyes. Then, he steps back into the protection of the shadows.

Steeling myself, I shrug my bow into my grasp, slipping an arrow into the nocking point. Without leaving myself time to reconsider, I step out of the shadows onto the rock plateau, which, to my left, hangs a short distance above the swamps. To my right, there is a cliff face.

I am now in Sindir's domain.

But it is not the darkness or the icy dread that encases me as I hover here that tells me whose realm I stand within. It is the black obsidian castle that towers before me, its powerful structure built upon the mountainside.

It was the castle of the High King before he was overthrown. Now, it lies dormant, the walls split by fissures that threaten the stability of the palace. Greenery climbs the sides, seeping in and out of the cracks and curling around the shattered windows, a symbol of its dormancy, of the time it has been left to rot, left in ruin.

Or so it was believed.

From where I stand, I catch sight of a cobblestone bridge running from one of the castle entrances and into the mountains, likely a passage to the city, which lies deep in the mountains, encased by a circle of towering hills. I have not seen it for myself, yet have heard rumours of the place where Orathin's citizens resided. Before its ruin, bridges were constructed to allow passage between the castle and city.

Lowering myself, I edge across the plateau, bow trained on the swamps before me, which expand into the distance. I search the expanse of space, which is cast in glimmers of silver light, for any signs of movement. For the burly figure of a racai, for the flame of a torch, for the glow of Valindor's gem.

Yet there is nothing.

I touch my tongue to the inside of my cheek in frustration, turning to the hillside ahead, yet it is too far away to clearly distinguish any figures that may lurk there. Lowering my bow, I search the space around me, and when I am sure I am alone, I inch towards the edge. Stopping before the ragged ledge, I lower myself onto my stomach, the cold of the stone seeping through the fabric of my clothes and into my skin, goosebumps trailing down my spine. The iridescent tip of my arrow shimmers in the moonlight as I move it across the expanse of the swamplands, but there is nothing.

I am alone.

A tremor rakes my body.

Am I too late?

My heart plummets at the thought.

Carefully drawing myself away from the edge, I move onto my knees, scanning the area before me, bow lowered. I chew on my lip, unsure how to proceed. I could continue, move further into his domain, towards the towering mountains at the edges of the swamp, through the wetlands, yet what would I find? The land before me is open, and although it would leave my enemy exposed, I, too, would be uncovered.

If the racai were here, I would know.

Anxiety coiling in my stomach, I bring myself to stand, arrow loose in the bow's hold. Stepping back, I prepare to venture further into Orathin.

A rough hand covers my mouth, hauling me away from the edge. Surprised, I act quickly, jamming my elbow backwards into my captor's stomach.

A low growl erupts from my enemy.

*Racai.*

I swivel around, knocking the beast onto the hard stone. My arrow slips free of the string, yet as it punctures the creature's heart, I am drawn backwards by a burly arm wrapped unforgivingly around my waist. My bow is torn from my grasp and kicked across the cold stone. I throw my head back, slamming it into the racai's, but it is futile, and stars blot my vision as another hand covers my mouth. I continue to fight the beast, yet it overpowers me. The more I struggle, the harder its nails sink into my skin, drawing blood.

Dragging me backwards, I continue to fight, throwing my elbows into its side, stomach, anywhere I can reach. Sinking my nails into any exposed flesh I can find, trying over and over to break free of its hold, yet there is nothing I can do. I am far too weak against this beast.

There is nothing I can do as I am dragged towards the cliff face, into a crevice etched into its towering frame, a passage.

Nothing I can do but let this beast drag me into the mountain.

Into Sindir's lair.

# PART TWO

WOVEN HEARTS

# TWENTY-TWO
## THALIA

I am hauled through a series of dark, stone corridors, much colder and crueller than that of Lsthrain. The ceilings are arched, and torches flicker alongside me, the flames casting my struggling shadow onto the walls, heightening my panic and the tinge of anger in my belly. My frustrated, fearful cries are muffled by the racai's coarse palm, closed firmly over my mouth.

Eventually, we stumble into a rectangular room, where two spacious cells mark the walls on my left. The door is open, and although I resist, I have no power over the beast when it shoves me into the prison. I catch myself before I am able to fall. Whirling towards the beast, I rush forward, but it slams the door shut before I can escape.

Its charred, red lips curve into a vile smirk, and I fight the revulsion churning my stomach. The key twists inside the lock, and when he pulls it free, he dangles it before me, teasing.

Despite the urge to reach for it, I remain still, chin held high, eyes locked on the beasts. I will not allow it the satisfaction of my desperation.

When it realises I shall not take the bait, it lowers the keys, a deep snarl parting its lips. It flips the key in the air, catching it in the opposite

150

hand before turning, departing through the corridor ahead, which is lined with dim cells.

I watch it vanish around the bend.

Releasing a breath, my body sags as I step backwards against the cold wall. I sink to the ground, drawing my knees against my chest.

I cannot deny the fear coursing through my veins, yet my determination is stronger.

I am here, in Sindir's stronghold. Surrounded by the beasts I have been fighting for these past days.

Surrounded by the beasts that have brought my life to this, to my sitting in an icy dungeon, one of which is hidden from the world. Nobody knows such a place exists, for the people believe the story as it has been told, of Sindir's death, of the palace and village of Orathin lying dormant. They do not know of his lair, hidden within the mountains in order to remain a secret.

Surrounded by the beasts that burned Enia, the kingdom where Calivar, the man who is like a father to me, resided. They took him from me. They have taken so much from me, so many lives and happiness.

They took my father from me.

Calivar and his kingdom.

*Killian.*

And I am tired of fighting them.

They may take from me, but I refuse for this to be a one-sided bargain. A give and take.

They may take from me, but I, too, shall take from them.

# TWENTY-THREE
## THALIA

ours into the night, I remain alone in my cell, back pressed against the rough wall, twirling a dragon-tip arrow within my grasp.

I have not been visited once. Have not been brought food nor water. No guard stands beyond my cell to watch over me.

At first, I was terrified, the reality of being in Sindir's realm, trapped in a cell within his stronghold, had crushed and petrified me to my core.

Now, I feel nothing but rage and determination.

I came here for a reason, and I shall not leave until that is satisfied.

A heavy thud echoes through the hollow space, and I drop my arrow, hauling myself onto my feet. At the end of the corridor, two racai round the corner, burly and twice my size.

I set my jaw and lift my chin, ignoring the inkling of fear that remains. It is nothing against the emotions waging war inside of me.

When they halt before my cell, I remain still, studying their movements and the weapons sheathed at their sides. The door clicks open, and they motion for me to come forward. I do not move.

"Where are you taking me?"

The racai before me smiles slowly, lips twitching. They do not respond, yet its wicked grin is answer enough.

I step out of the cell.

Roughly, each beast takes one of my arms, the swords at their hips pressing ruthlessly into my sides. As they begin to walk, I fall into stride with them.

I do not resist. Do not complain as their weapons dig into my skin, as their nails sink into the flesh of my arms, as they tug me roughly around the corners, take the stairs three at a time so that I trip as we ascend the steps.

I do not resist.

I allow them to lead me to Sindir.

We tread through more of the dark corridors, many lined with imposing wooden doors, stained a black as dark as the night sky and embellished with patterns of gold.

Eventually, we arrive at a large, circular foyer, complete with high ceilings. The floor is a black marble, inset with traces of sparkling gold. Two curved staircases are set on either side of the room, joining together at a platform that hovers above me. The entrance doors are tall, twice the height of average ones; they rest to my left, matching those we had passed earlier.

They take a sharp turn, dragging me to the right, where a towering arch lies opposite the entrance doors.

My breath catches as we pass into the room.

The throne room.

The ceiling is that of two levels, held up by a line of pillars on either side of the gold carpet, which rolls through the centre of the room to the dais at its end. The pillars are pure black, twisted and curved, inset with ridges and crevices, much like the vines Killian and I encountered within the undying forest.

I shift my gaze slowly, reluctantly, for I know what shall lie before me.

At the end of the shimmering gold carpet is a dais of pure black, a matching throne upon it. Shadows flutter about the seat, a beautiful and dreadful dance of darkness.

Yet it is the figure upon the throne that my gaze settles on.

With a long, black cloak that drapes over the steps of the dais and a plate of immaculate silver armour, the shoulders curved up and outwards, sharp enough to pierce skin. Jagged points protrude from different areas of the armour in a wordless threat and warning of this man's nature.

Ruthless.

Merciless.

Sindir, king of Orathin.

I feel the fear coiling at the bottom of my stomach once more, heavy and consuming. The urge to fight these beasts, to escape from this man, overwhelms me, yet I do not heed the warning. Instead, I tilt my chin and set my shoulders, keeping my gaze fixed on the king to appear undaunted.

I will not fear this man.

As we halt near the base of the dais, I am able to study him more closely. His jaw is sharp enough to draw blood, with an almost triangular set to it, and his cheekbones are high, shadowed by the darkness of his pitch-black hair, which has a slight wave to it.

When my eyes find his, I notice he has been studying me as I have him. His eyes are a dark, piercing blue, yet they flicker, darkness shrouding them as shadows dance about his pupils. A single scar is etched beneath his left eye, a barely noticeable raised line.

In truth, he is frightening, with the sort of attractiveness that implies danger.

"She was found scouting the swamplands," one of the racai growls.

Sindir does not say a word and instead continues to study me, his gaze boring into my own.

"Will you bow to your king?" His voice is impossibly deep, threatening as it booms through this quiet, hollow room.

I remain silent, not daring to break his gaze.

The racai to my left growls, slicing its nails through the skin on my arm. A sharp sting echoes in response to the warm trickle of blood.

I do not move, do not let my gaze falter.

The darkness within his eyes grows, eating away at the blue. "*Bow. To. Your. King.*"

When I make no attempt to do so, the racai shift to grip my shoulders, slamming me onto the unyielding marble floor. The connection makes my knees crack, and I grit my teeth against the pain.

Sindir's eyes flit over me, scanning my face, the weapons at my waist. He tips his head, and the racai remove my daggers and the quiver across my back, tossing them to the side, out of my reach.

After a moment, he stands, stretching to his full, imposing height. He moves away from the throne, taking the steps one at a time, slowly, curiously. Each move is calculated, like a predator stalking its prey. When he halts before me, his head tilts to the side, eyes flashing dangerously.

"Who are you?"

My eyebrows twitch in contemplation, and I take a few moments to decide upon my next words.

"I am no one."

His eyebrow quirks.

"Is that so?"

I do not reply.

"Then why is it you have entered my domain?"

"I came for Valindor."

His eyebrows raise, and he glances at the racai. When his gaze returns to mine, a low, humourless chuckle escapes his lips.

"You truly believe a lowly girl such as yourself could steal Valindor from beneath my sights without my noticing?"

I angle my head to the side. "I believe if you could overthrow your brother, the high king, and steal his throne, I could steal a sword from your stronghold."

His eyes darken further as he stares down at me, towering, intimidating, yet I do not cower in his presence. "Foolish girl." His lips are curved to one side, a slight smirk. "You failed."

He turns away from me, cloak swishing with the movement, yet before he can ascend the dais, I jerk myself free of the beasts, leaping to my feet. They grab my shoulders, pulling me back against them, but it does not stop me from calling to Sindir.

"You took something of mine."

Without stopping, he replies, "I have taken many things."

"You took my father from me."

He halts yet does not turn to face me.

"Many lives I have taken. What makes you think you are any different?"

"I am not," I reply, fighting the racai's grasp.

For a moment, he is silent. Then, he turns to face me, studying me with dangerous eyes before moving towards me once more, halting in the spot before me.

"What is your name?"

I tip my chin up, meeting his shadowy gaze. "Thalia Valeikka."

He grows rigid, the entirety of his powerful figure tensing at my words. The blue is now gone from his eyes, the shadows more defined. His demeanour changes into something I cannot decipher, and for a few long moments, he just studies me, eyes flitting rapidly over my face, a muscle pulsing in his neck.

"Kneel."

Pressure is applied to my shoulder, attempting to force me down once more, but I resist.

"Kneel before your *king*," he seethes.

I lean forward so that my face is mere inches from his own. My jaw is set, teeth gritted. "You. Are. No. *King*."

Before I may continue, the sword at his hip is drawn, the tip of his blade pressed against my shoulder to force me to my knees. He drags the blade to my throat and tilts my chin up with its tip, forcing me to meet his menacing gaze.

"Here is what you shall do," he drawls. "I shall allow you to live if you do something for me in return." His head tilts. "You will return to your people and deliver a message for me."

"Why should I do anything for you?" I spit.

His lips curl, revealing his bared teeth, and he drags the blade down, purposefully slow, to where it rests against my collarbone.

"Because." He allows the tip to dig into my flesh, and I suck in a sharp breath as he drags the tip across my skin, drawing a perfect line just below my bone. Warmth blossoms in the path of the blade, and I lower my eyes to see the familiar crystal-red of elven blood staining my flesh. "If you do not, your people shall not foresee it. I intend on bringing war to these lands, and what fun is it if your enemies are so unprepared they cannot put up a fight?"

I bring my gaze back to his. "You are *depraved*."

A wicked grin touches his lips. "Yes, I am, *Thalia*."

My name on his lips makes my stomach churn with nausea.

I long to defy him, yet I cannot deny how foolish it would be. No matter how much I wish to disobey him, I cannot withhold this information from my people.

If I do, Ilya will fall beneath Sindir's rule within a matter of days.

158

Cities will be burned, homes will be raided, and the number of lives lost shall be insurmountable.

His gaze shifts to the racai, and he tips his head to the side, motioning to my discarded weapons. "Give them to her. She will not resist if she wishes to try and save these lands, however futile her attempt may be. Besides, we do not want her killed before she can return to her kingdom, do we?"

Biting back a bitter remark, I hold his gaze, determined not to break it, to show any sign of weakness, even as his piercing, shadowed eyes bore into my own. Even as the racai retrieve my quiver and daggers, then slip them back into place.

As the beasts haul me onto my feet, I lift my chin, fully aware of the blood staining my collarbone, of the mounting pain.

"You underestimate me."

He leans forward, breath hot against my cheek, and I am forced to conceal my disgust. "And yet who stands before you, a crown upon his head? *Who* is detained? *Who* is in power?"

Before I can say another word, I am dragged backwards, and then spun around to face the foyer. Behind me, Sindir's footsteps echo, growing distant.

The racai drag me through another series of tunnels, hauling me sharply around corners and forcing me up stairs. We pass more of the beasts as we move, all of which scrutinise me with their beady eyes. I do not give them the satisfaction of fear, instead focusing on our movements, on the corridors we tread through, tread past, at the doors that line each hallway. I study them, study the path we take, the directions we turn—*every* detail of our journey.

Something catches my eye.

It is but a mere set of double doors, an almost perfect match to the rest that line these dim corridors.

Yet this one is different—a small, almost insignificant detail, yet remarkable enough to catch my eye.

A small, gold skull backed by two jagged blades, which are crossed behind it and built into the handles. It is an intricate design, small yet definitive. A minor detail to better define this room.

Sindir's quarters.

If Valindor is to be anywhere, it shall be there. He is not foolish enough to leave it somewhere of easy access, no matter how few know of this place or his being alive.

As we continue to walk, I note our path until I have memorised our entire journey by the time we reach a dank tunnel.

Here, the ceiling is much lower, and the air is filled with a menacing chill. There are no torches. The corridor stretches forward, and as I squint through the dark, I am able to make out a stone door at its end.

My exit.

When we reach the end, the racai shove me forward, the force of their strength making me stumble. I quickly regain myself, touching my tongue to the inside of my cheek in frustration as I cast them a furious glance over my shoulder. They motion to the stone door, an almost imperceptible outline in the mountainside.

"So this is it?" I ask.

One of them growls, the sound ricocheting off the cold mountain walls. "You wish to stay?"

I turn toward them, tilting my head in mock innocence as I survey the beasts. "Indeed. I have not yet gotten what I came for."

In one swift movement, my daggers are free, plunged straight through the exposed flesh of the racai, where their armour does not reach. I twist the blades, quickly withdrawing them before spinning around their falling bodies. Blood darkens the ground as I stare at their lifeless forms; the light dulled from their eyes, not a sound made.

Wiping the blood from my blades upon their armour, I step back, then slip my daggers into their scabbards. Turning back down the tunnel, I move to the edge of the passage, hand set protectively upon the hilt of my blade. Halting before the bend, I press myself into the rock, listening for any signs of my enemy, but it is silent.

Fingers curling around the hilt of my dagger, I take a steadying breath before stepping out of the dim tunnel. I examine my surroundings, checking that I am alone. When I am confident in my solitude, I continue to move through the corridors, examining every bend, slipping into shadowed hallways and empty rooms to avoid the beasts. A few times, I am nearly caught, yet I manage to evade the racai with my quick thinking and the advanced senses of an elf.

As I round the last bend to Sindir's quarters, my hand falls away from my dagger, and I scuttle to the opposite side of the corridor, where the door lies.

A voice echoes through the hall.

I halt immediately, my hand hovering above the handle. To my right, voices ricochet off the walls, accompanied by footsteps, growing closer. Desperate, I try the handle, yet the doors are locked. Cursing beneath my breath, I slip around a corner into a blackened hall. Pressing myself flush against the wall, I conceal myself within the shadows.

The footsteps cease, halting just around the corner at the entrance to Sindir's quarters. I hold my breath, afraid that even the most insignificant of movements shall grasp his attention, for he is not a foolish man. There is a click and the shift of a door. The voices resume, yet they speak in a language of dark origin, something only Sindir and his creatures understand.

Before I can react, a Blood Rider strides past, its long gown rippling behind it.

I freeze, breath hitching in my throat, yet to my relief, it does not notice me and quickly vanishes from sight.

Now, I am stuck within Sindir's domain, desperate to find Valindor, which I am sure is kept within his quarters.

The quarters that he is in.

Yet I cannot wait, cannot linger here, for I do not have such time.

Nor can I leave without Valindor.

I have no more time to waste, no choice.

Once again checking the corridor, I slide out of the shadows, creeping to the door of his quarters. This time, when I try the handle, it is unlocked. Steadying myself, I push it open a few inches, just enough to peer inside.

I freeze when Sindir's towering figure treads past, graceful despite his heavy build, as he vanishes through an archway.

Steeling myself with a breath, I push the door open and slip inside.

# TWENTY-FOUR

## THALIA

he room is cold. Barren.

As soon as I am inside, a chill slips over me, and my body is riddled with merciless goosebumps.

The contents of the room are meagre. There is a bed before me, four times the size of what I occupy in Lsthrain. It is neatly made with pure black sheets and decorative pillows, a gold rug beneath it. On either side of the bed is a side table, and against one of the walls is a wardrobe, a vanity at its side. A single candlestick and gold embellished black skull lies upon it. A shiver rakes my spine, and I force myself to move away from the door, allowing it to click quietly into place behind me.

I edge across the wall, hand resting upon the hilt of my blade as I hide before the arch where Sindir vanished into, pressing my body into the wall. Cautiously, I peer around the corner.

He stands in the centre of the room, which is much less vacant than his sleeping quarters, with various ornaments and weapons scattered throughout the space. Large windows are set into two of the stone walls; black curtains pulled to the side to allow the moonlight to cascade in.

Few candles burn throughout the room, casting it in a fiery silver glow and glancing off the few gold embellishments.

Sindir stands hunched over an oval table, staring down at something I cannot make out. He no longer wears his plate of armour and instead dons a loose black shirt, revealing a slice of the muscles that line his body, an intimidation of his strength and power. His brows are drawn, eyes dancing with shadows and fingers splayed across the table.

Resting within the scabbard at his hip is Valindor.

My teeth sink into my lip as I stare at the gleaming sword, fingers curled around the hilt of my own blade as I contemplate my next move.

He straightens himself, then turns towards me.

I jerk away from the arch, out of his view.

His footsteps echo towards me, in sync with the rapid beat of my heart.

I have nowhere to go. Nowhere to hide.

I am trapped.

Squeezing my eyes shut, I inhale shakily, trying to calm my ragged breaths and the unsteady beat of my heart as I prepare myself for what I am about to do.

He steps through the arch, and I free my dagger, slamming it through his gut in one rapid motion. His eyes widen, darting to me, full lips parted in shock. Without awaiting a response, I kick him against the wall, thrusting the edge of my blade against his throat, as he had done to me.

In a matter of seconds, I have freed Valindor from his sheath, and I hold it before me, its tip pressed against the place of his heart.

If he has one.

I lean forward, teeth bared as I drag my dagger down the line of his throat, careful not to nick his skin. I flatten the blade's edge below his collarbone, and my eyes snag on a faint scar that already mars his skin. It is in the same place he had drawn the line across my collarbone, and I feel confusion seep in. I shake it off, unable to afford a distraction. My lips twist into a smug smile as I stare up at him, my head tilted to meet his wicked gaze from where he towers over me, easily a head or two taller than I. I drag the blade across his flesh, applying enough pressure for the line to scar. Blood flows over his smooth skin, soaking into the black of his shirt.

"*Who* is in power now?" I seethe.

Before he can respond, I crack the hilt of my dagger upon his skull. And then I run.

I stagger through the door, slamming it behind me and using one of my sturdy dragon-tip arrows to bolt it closed. The doors jolt violently as he throws himself against it, and I stumble back, the arrow threatening to snap, despite its strength. Sindir's shouts echo throughout the empty corridor, and I take off.

A thunderous bang ricochets off the walls, the doors swinging open violently. I do not stop. Do not stop when his shouts reach my ears, nor when they follow me down the corridor. I do not stop when the footfalls of his followers fill the space behind me, do not stop when arrows zip past, narrowly missing me, do not stop when my lungs burn, and my legs grow weak.

I stop only when I round a corner, free of the racai's sights, and duck into one of the many hallways.

My breaths are quick, rapid, and I try my best to conceal them, to quiet myself, but it is near futile, for I am too breathless to slow my intake of air.

The footfalls slow, and a racai steps into view, its lips curling as it scans the area, a growl rising in its throat.

The space is too quiet, my breathing too loud.

The racai's head snaps towards me, and I step free of the shadows, whirling around the beast before jamming my elbow against its throat and digging Valindor between its shoulder blades.

It drops without a sound.

For a moment, I stand, blade held loosely at my side as I try to slow my breathing and calm the racing of my pulse.

More shouts echo from the surrounding corridors, and I have no choice but to continue running. Sprinting down a connecting hall, I find the tunnel I had earlier been led to, where the racai's bodies remain. I throw myself against the door, and it swings open. I stumble out into the cold night air.

My breath hitches as I catch myself on a thin ledge.

Fear rolls through my body at the sight before me.

I am suspended high above the plateaus, alone on a tiny ledge.

And the only way down is to climb.

I glance behind me, the racai's enraged shouts reaching me, even from where I stand.

Having no choice, I turn to the corridor, Valindor tight in my hand as I drop onto my stomach and lower myself over the edge. Quickly finding a foothold, I grasp the jagged rock, which slices through my skin, causing my palms to bleed, yet the pain, like that on my collarbone, is distant, for the fear overrides my senses.

Lower and lower, I climb, constantly faced with the fear of falling, of being struck with an arrow from above. On a few occasions, my grasp slips, and a strangled cry escapes me as I scramble for a foothold. At one point, my foot catches on a jutting stone, slicing into my leg, but nevertheless, saving me from falling, I press my cheek against the cold rock, holding myself against it as I try to regain my breath.

When I finally pull away, glancing at the stone platform below me, my fear tamps down, if only slightly. I have descended the majority of the cliff face.

"*There!*"

My heart lurches, and I raise my head, nails digging into the mountainside. Above me, a horde of racai are gathered, their weapons drawn, arrows aimed for me.

I look away, making my body flush with the stone to avoid the path of their arrows, but even as they shoot past me, I realise they are too close. They will not miss again.

I turn away, glancing below me, limbs trembling with fright. Chest heaving, I tighten my grip on Valindor's hilt, knuckles turning a ghostly white.

And then I jump.

# TWENTY-FIVE
## THALIA

land smoother than I expect, somersaulting to avoid the flurry of arrows from above. When their firing comes to a halt, I look up to where they are hastily reloading their bows, but by the time they are ready to strike, I am already gone, sprinting across the wide plateau, straight for the forest in the distance, where Alwyne is hidden.

Their arrows follow me as I run, striking dangerously close to my heels. The tips bounce off the stone, shattering from the force of their strikes. As I near the border of the forest, I duck down without slowing my pace, retrieving my discarded bow from earlier, before the racai had stolen me into Sindir's lair.

Before the arrows can hurt me, I vanish into the tree line, although I do not stop. I continue running, my breathing ragged and my legs on fire as I leap over downed logs and manoeuvre the uneven ground.

I stumble to a halt when I reach the place of Alwyne's hiding, and I stagger into the bush, reaching for his saddle to support me. Inhaling sharply, my breath catches, for there is too little air in my body. Nonetheless, I haul myself onto Alwyne's back, taking the reins in one hand whilst holding Valindor in the other.

I have not the time to catch my breath, for the beast's shouts echo throughout the eerie wood.

I tap Alwyne's side, and he takes off, galloping through the dense wood as fast as the sprawling roots and mangled bushes allow.

Eventually, their furious howls fade, taken away by the wind, and my breathing returns to normal. Only when there are no traces of the beast's furious howls, when I know we are alone and a safe distance from Orathin and Sindir's beast's do I allow Alwyne to slow. My body sags, and I lean forward, pressing myself flush against Alwyne's neck as I wrap my arms around him, careful with the blade still in my hand. My body trembles with relief, and I find a small smile curling my lips, which I hide against Alwyne's soft mane. I inhale deeply, exhaling with the comfort that Valindor is in my possession once more.

Alwyne whinnies, shaking his head, and I close my eyes against his soft, dark mane, exhaustion clawing at me once more. It is only now, when the adrenaline has worn off, that I start to feel the full weight of my injuries. The cut at my collarbone is throbbing, the surrounding skin stained with my blood, although it is dry. The gash is shallow but enough to scar. Still, it does not ease the pain. I sit up, reaching back to slip Valindor into my quiver, which is large enough to hold both the sword and my arrows. Hands empty, I flip them over, examining my blood-coated palms and the thin scratches that mar my skin, evidence of my climb. My leg aches, yet only slightly, the consequence of my near-fall upon the cliff face, although no blood stains my pant leg.

My stomach grumbles, and I place my hand upon it, trying to ease the painful emptiness. I must find a place to rest before I worry about such a thing.

I click my tongue, taking the reins back into hand. Alwyne obeys, moving into a canter.

*

It is but a short time after I departed Orathin, when the beast's cries are long gone that I am startled by an eruption of birds. A flock explodes from the trees, their eerie cries echoing in the wood as they spiral against the night sky, then disappear into the darkness.

I tug the reins, halting abruptly as my gaze searches the shadows, wary. My fingers coil about the hilt of my dagger as a branch snaps to my left, then ahead. The blade slips free of the scabbard with a smooth, silky sound, and I adjust my grip.

A whoosh of air tousles my hair, and my dagger is knocked from my hand, followed by a shattering sound.

Instinctively, I lower my body, slipping free of the stirrups and dropping to the forest floor in a graceful somersault, dragging my other dagger free. My gaze drops to the blade that lies on the ground. It remains intact, yet beside it rests the shaft of an arrow, its shattered head spilt around it.

Leaves crunch beneath heavy boots, and I lurch to my feet, spinning around my opponent before they may strike. Another rushes me, and my blade connects with another, sparks igniting in the darkness. My eyes clash with my rivals, and shock coils in my stomach.

It is not one of Orathin's beasts but rather a human.

My lips part in a mere second of distraction, yet it is enough for my foe to gain the upper hand. The dagger is knocked from my grasp, and I duck beneath the swing of a blade, rolling behind them and kicking my leg out to knock them off balance. They crash to the ground, curved sword lodging into the dirt. I reach forward, gripping it tightly.

I am hauled backwards by my hair, and sharp pain tugs at my scalp as I cry out, the blade slipping from my grasp. Pulled onto my feet, I throw my elbow backwards, the connection with soft flesh followed by a grunt. I whirl, my gaze snagging on the surrounding trees, lined with archers.

Arrows trained on me from all directions.

There are too many.

An arm snakes around my waist, and I am jerked backwards until my back connects with the rough bark of a tree. A face comes into view, and I feel the merciless cold of a blade against my skin. The man towers over me, with deadly black eyes and a dark stubble, shaggy hair and a broad build. I tilt my head back against the tree, trying to escape the cool nick of the blade; my gaze narrowed as it remains locked on his, refusing to back down.

"Care to tell me who you are, or shall we stay here for the remainder of the night?" He asks, voice deadly quiet.

"My identity is my own. I care not how long we stand here; it is of no consequence to me. I am not the one who shall tire of holding that blade."

A shadow creeps along his jaw, and a muscle pulses in his neck, yet he does not humour my response. Instead, another voice rings out.

"Who are you?"

I tilt my head just enough so the blade cannot slice my skin. Behind the man, a woman approaches. She wears her brown hair in an intricately braided half up-half down do, with a splotch of black paint circling her right eye. A coat of fur dons her shoulders, intimidating blades sheathed at her side. Had she been an elf, I would suspect her of being a few years older than I.

"I ask the same of you."

The blade is pressed into my skin, and I regard the man with a glare.

She clicks her tongue, drawing closer. "Brave girl." Her head tilts. "Or is it but a show? There is fear in your eyes."

A bitter laugh escapes my lips, the night's events heightening my anger of this encounter, for it is but a mere nuisance after what I have faced, another obstacle before my goal. I do not fear these people, *especially* after the troubles of the past few days.

"I do not *fear* you. You are but a mere inconvenience to me, a group of travellers in a realm far beyond your comprehension, and I assure you, I have encountered much worse than you."

Her lips press into a thin line. "I highly doubt that."

"Doubt is often the cause for one's defeat."

I thrust my knee into the man's stomach, gaining myself a brief opening as the blade slips. Catching the man's wrist, I twist it behind his back, capturing the sword before it may hit the ground and slamming him against the tree so that the rough bark digs into his cheek. I press the blade to the side of his throat.

173

"*Doubt* is your enemy, not I. There are things that roam this forest you have only ever heard of in the stories."

The woman's eyes are darker now, less doubtful, more serious. "And what is that?"

I shake my head. "You would not believe me."

She is silent for a moment. Then, she tips her head towards the archers, and I tighten my grip upon the blade, a warning not to fire, and to my surprise, they do not. Instead, the arrows are lowered, slipped free of their notchings, and I startle when she tosses me my daggers. They land on the ground before me, and I cast them a sceptical glance before turning my gaze back to the woman, the leader of the group.

She returns my stare, expressionless as she speaks. "The racai, that is what you speak of."

My eyes narrow, caught off guard. I should not be surprised, considering our whereabouts and close proximity to Orathin. Yet after the scepticism I received when telling others of my encounters, I would not expect another to believe in their reappearance.

Yet she does, for it is clear that she, too, has encountered them.

Before me, the man shifts, an attempt to escape the blade, yet I press it harder against his skin, baring my teeth against the ire boiling in my stomach. I have grown tired of these obstacles. I wish only to rid myself of this place and return to Lsthrain, where I shall fight alongside my kingdom.

"Do. Not. *Move*," I growl.

"Tell me that is what you speak of?" I turn my attention back to the woman, giving her a quick once over, searching for signs of a lie, yet nothing seems as though she speaks anything but the truth.

Reluctantly, I drop the blade from the man's throat, tossing it down, where the tip lodges into the soil. I step away from him, reaching for my daggers before straightening my spine.

I can feel the anger radiating from the man, the tension rolling off him in violent waves, and a smirk tugs at my lips.

The swell of pride never ceases when I prove to those who deem me unworthy as their equal.

I level my gaze with the leaders. "Yes, it is."

"You have encountered them?"

"And Blood Riders, many times."

A hushed silence falls over the travellers at my response, and I allow my gaze to wander, to take in their wide eyes and inquisitive glances.

"And you, have you crossed paths with the beasts?" I ask.

She dips her head. "Briefly. We managed to evade them with little trouble, although we suffered a few injuries."

"You should not be in this part of the woods; it is too dangerous a territory. I suggest you find another path to travel upon, lest you encounter them again."

Her brows lift, and she takes a step closer. "Who are you to tell us how we should continue our journey?"

"No one. I am merely warning you of the risk."

"Then why is it you are here, travelling in the darkness with those beasts prowling the area, *alone?*"

"My matter is my own," I reply firmly.

One side of her mouth ticks up. "As stubborn as you are brave." She tips her head to the archers, and I watch as they begin to disperse.

"Come, join us. We have extra food, and you cannot leave such a wound unattended." The leader waves her hand at the line of blood smearing my collarbone.

For a moment, I do not move, watching the group of travellers vanishing into the trees with scrutiny. The leader disappears into the darkness, and I startle when the man steps up beside me, having forgotten he was there.

I level him with a cautious look, one that he returns with an edge of humour, which tugs at his lips. "I shall give it to you; that move was quite unexpected."

"Exactly why it worked."

He tries to conceal his grin but fails. Tipping his head towards the trees, he retrieves his blade. "Come."

I watch as he begins forward, following after the leader. "And why should I trust you?"

He pauses, pivoting his body to face me, a small, genuine smile gracing his lips. "Because we share a common enemy, and believe me, had we wanted you dead, you would be dead."

*

The fire crackles before me, sparks erupting into the chilly night air and casting a warm orange glow over the trees. Despite the warmth the fire brings, I cannot rid myself of the fear that settles in the pit of my stomach. It is doubtful the racai have given up in their search for me and Valindor, and I worry that the flames shall draw them to us. I said as such when I first saw the fire, yet gained no response from the travellers and have thus decided to drop it. Foolish it may be, but I cannot refuse this offering of warmth and security that both the fire and this group of travellers bring. Nevertheless, I refuse to let my guard down, for I do not know them and hence cannot fully trust them, yet it is their kindness, hospitality and the man's words that continue to play in my mind that gives me a semblance of trust.

*Believe me, had we wanted you dead, you would be dead.*

However dire his words may be, they ring true.

"Here."

I tip my head up, locking gazes with the man I had earlier encountered, the one who had detained me. Ryhan. He holds his hand out, a wooden bowl within his grasp. When I hesitate, he sighs, dropping down onto the log beside me and motioning for me to take it.

"As I said—"

"Had you wanted me dead, I would already be so," I repeat, surprised to find a small smile gracing my lips.

His lips tip up in response. "Correct."

I stare down at the soup. It is a simple broth with a few vegetables bobbing at its surface. Nevertheless, I am grateful for such a meal. Hesitantly, I pick up the spoon, bringing a mouthful of the soup to my lips. There is little flavour, but I care not. The nourishment alone shall be enough to spur me on for these last dregs of my journey.

I look back to Ryhan as he eats his soup, watching the flames leap and dance, crackling. "Thank you."

He bows his head. "My pleasure."

For the majority of my meal, I observe the camp. Covered wagons are set throughout the tight area, and the travellers bustle back and forth, chatting and laughing with one another whilst enjoying their meal. Their wagons are specially crafted for journeys beyond a beaten path, ones that are easily able to navigate the uneven forest grounds without need of a trail. My gaze snags on Alwyne, who is being attended to alongside the other horses, being nourished with both the food and drink he has been lacking.

Once I have finished my soup, the leader, whose name I have learned is Alaida, leads me to one of the wagons, motioning for me to join her inside. She leaves me to the physician, who greets me with a welcoming smile, her long black hair swaying as she moves around, gathering what she needs to clean my wounds. As she tends to my injuries, she asks me a few questions, seeming not to interrogate me but to ask with curiosity.

When the wounds are clean and free from the risk of infection, I am led to a supply wagon, where there is a spare built-in bed. The supplies that once sat upon it have now been moved, leaving me with a comfortable place to sleep. The bed is narrow, yet it is nothing I am not used to and is a luxury out here.

Slowly, I turn to face Alaida, who stands by the entrance of this cramped space.

"I apologise, your—" I hesitate. "Hospitality— after our initial meeting — has meant a lot to me." Her lips curve upwards at my words. "But I cannot stay. These woods are far too dangerous for me to linger within, and I must return to my kingdom. I cannot delay."

She clicks her tongue, crossing her arms over her chest. "That is unwise."

"I care not. There are people that need me, people I care for."

Alaida sighs, leaning back against the entranceway, sympathy creeping into her eyes. "I understand, yet you can be of no use to them if you are drained of energy."

"I know my limits."

"And you choose to push them?" She asks, raising her brows. "I do not know your story, yet for you to be alone in *these* woods at night? With such injuries? I cannot imagine you have had a desirable time. Sleep a few hours, it is for the best, and not much time shall be wasted."

"But it *will* be wasted," I reply stubbornly. "And it is time I cannot afford to slip away."

Her eyes flutter closed, her jaw tightening with frustration. "I am not unfamiliar with the toll a journey can take on you. Not only the physical exertion—" she waves to my tended wound. "But alongside the injuries and mental toll, it drains you, weakens you. I try not to hinder you but to aid you. Take it from someone who knows the consequences of continuing when you ought to stop."

I swallow thickly, averting my gaze.

Despite my fear, I know Alaida is right, yet I cannot banish the thought of losing anyone or anything else.

Cannot banish the thought of losing Killian for good.

A lump forms in my throat at the notion, and I perch gently on the bed, gripping the edge with ghostly white knuckles.

"I understand you, Thalia. I truly do." This time, Alaida's voice is gentler, her eyes softer. "But please, do yourself a favour and sleep, if only for a few hours."

I catch my lip between my teeth, brushing my fingers over the soft blanket beneath me. In truth, I am exhausted, and I know I shall not be able to keep the exhaustion at bay for much longer. With a reluctant nod, I bring my gaze back to hers.

"All right."

Alaida nods, pushing away from the wall. "You can stay with us for as long as you please, know you are welcome."

I force my lips to curve, although the warmth flooding my chest at her kindness is genuine. "Thank you, Alaida."

She dips her chin before disappearing. "Goodnight."

*

It takes me a while to fall asleep, for I cannot seem to shut my mind off, to keep from startling at every slight, unexpected sound. The distant snap of a branch, crackle of the fire or laughter of those who remain outside, keeping watch over the camp. When I do drift off, it is only a few hours before I awaken again, shooting up in a panic, my hands grappling for the daggers that rest not at my hip but beside the petite bed.

A shudder rolls through my body, and I lay back down slowly, pulling the blanket higher and curling into it, grateful for the warmth and comfort it brings. Rolling onto my side, I stare at the dark outline of the supplies before me, stacked high to maximise the space. I force myself to close my eyes, painting over the unwanted images with memories from my past, good memories.

Yet no matter how hard I try, I cannot fall back into such a slumber.

Eyes wafting open, I bring myself to perch on the edge of the bed with a sigh. I tug my boots on and bring myself to stand, slipping my daggers into their sheaths, followed by my bow and quiver, which I cast over my back before departing the wagon.

The cool night air encases me, and a shiver rocks through my body, riddling my skin with goosebumps. I stand on the top step for a moment, scanning the camp until my gaze lands on the fire and the lone man beside it.

I descend the steps and make my way over. The chill seeps into my cloak but is unable to pierce my skin. Hesitantly, I take a seat on the log beside Ryhan, watching the fire. He does not acknowledge my presence at first, yet after a few moments, he speaks.

"Could not sleep?"

I shake my head. "Not any longer."

He is silent for a moment. "It would seem you have a lot on your mind."

A humourless laugh escapes my lips. "It would seem so."

"Things are changing. It feels as though—" he cuts himself off, and I turn to face him, squinting at the reflection of fire that dances across his jaw. "The peace is fracturing."

"Yes, it does," I reply quietly. I drop my gaze, contemplating.

"I do not know where you plan to travel, yet I can only advise you to find a different route if it involves you travelling North-East. We spotted the racai heading that way, and despite your bravery and skill, you alone could not fend off an entire horde of the beasts."

*North-East.*

An inkling of dread seeps into the pit of my stomach.

*Something is wrong.*

"North-East?"

He dips his chin. "Indeed."

*Now that the racai have Valindor, they will be rallying their forces against Lsthrain. They have an alliance with the trolls, if you recall.*

No.

I lurch to my feet, sprinting to Alwyne's side and fumbling with his ties.

"Hey! What is it? Thalia!"

I ignore Ryhan, swinging the reins over Alwyne's head and backing him out of the tight space alongside the other horses so that I may mount. As I grasp the pommel, Ryhan appears at my side, halting me.

"What are you doing?"

His features are drawn, a mixture of frustration and confusion.

"They head for my kingdom. They plan to bring it down."

He does not respond for a moment, fixated on a spot beyond me, and I see the moment it dawns on him the weight of my words. His eyes flicker back to mine, and he nods.

"I wish you all the best, Thalia. I think it is safe to speak for everyone, but it was a pleasure to meet you, and should you need anything in the future..." his lips curve. "I am sure you shall be able to find us. Know that we share a common enemy."

I nod rapidly, grateful for his words yet desperate to be on the move.

"Please, thank the rest of your accomplices for their hospitality," I pause. "Yours could have been better at the beginning."

A chuckle rises out of him, and I swing myself into the saddle, gathering the reins.

"Good luck, Thalia."

I bow my head, then click my tongue and take off into the dark forest.

*

It is but a few mere hours later that we break the border of the forest. In the distance lies Verila, the gates illuminated in the faint orange glow of candlelight.

Alwyne slows to a trot, allowing himself a small break. Nevertheless, he maintains a steady pace. I watch the kingdom as we pass through the field, studying its border and the shabby roofing, which peers over the top of the wall.

I reach down, grazing my hand over Alwyne's sweat-slicked neck. He raises his head, nickering softly, and I pat his soft coat, sending tufts of hair into the night air.

I urge Alwyne on, and he transitions into a gallop, the earth thudding beneath his hooves. The speed whips my hair away from my face, revealing my skin to the chilly air, and I close my eyes against it, allowing it to riddle goosebumps across my face. To feel something other than *pain*.

Although I have Valindor, I know this is far from over.

For the battle may be done.

But the war has only just begun.

# TWENTY-FIVE
## KILLIAN

unlight filters into the cave, flooding past my eyelids. I recoil, raising my arm to shield my eyes, which have begun to flutter open. Turning away from the sun, I brace my shoulder against the wall, blinking to clear my vision.

The cave walls are illuminated in yellow light casting both Elwis's and I's shadows upon them. I drop my arm, closing my eyes once more as yesterday's events rush to the forefront of my mind. Carefully, I roll up the sleeve of my shirt, revealing the bandaged gash on my forearm. I brush my fingers over the bandage and press lightly to test it. A wave of pain washes over me, and I hiss through my teeth, a vein in my arm pulsing from the sudden hurt. I drop my sleeve back down, supporting myself against the stone as I bring myself to stand.

Across the cave, Elwis whinnies, shaking her head to me, mane flowing wildly with the motion. My lips curve into a gentle smile, but it is not one of pure joy, but instead, one that is tamped down.

I pad over to her, running my hands over her nose in response. She snorts, and I pat her neck before dragging the reins over her head.

"Are you ready?" I ask, although I know she is just as exhausted as I and shall offer no response.

With the silence that follows my question, I lead her free of the cave, rounding the bend and halting before the slope Thalia and I had travelled. I slide my foot into the stirrup, grasping the pommel of the saddle and heaving myself into the leather seat. I click my tongue, and we begin our ascent up the steep slope. Leaning forward to better our balance, I twine my fingers through her mane for a sturdy grasp. When we crest the path, I lean back, straightening my posture and re-adjusting my grip on the reins.

Rays of golden light are cast over the mountain tops, streaming down the rock walls on either side of me.

It is a truly remarkable sight, yet I have not the will to appreciate it. Not now.

Especially when this place is nothing but fuel for memories, a reminder of the last time I was here.

With Thalia.

I urge Elwis to increase our pace, for I am desperate to be rid of this place.

*

We ride at a steady pace for the remainder of the mountain trail, and despite my reluctance, I follow the same path Thalia and I had taken for fear that if I choose a different path, I shall get lost within the hills.

It takes us only a few hours to reach the treacherous slope we had descended upon our arrival in Enia. I tug lightly on the reins, demanding Elwis to halt. She obeys, digging her hoof into the rough trail as we stand upon the cliffs, towering above what was once a beautiful kingdom, now

186

nothing but ruin.

The once magnificent, towering palace is nothing but a pile of charred rubble; the walls crumbled in upon themselves, their edges blackened by fire. Many of the bridges are destroyed, their wooden planks weakened by flames and snapped by the heat. They float through the crystal blue waters, a symbol of the battle that raged here not long ago.

My heart breaks.

It breaks for Calivar and his people.

It breaks for the lives lost.

It breaks for Thalia.

It breaks for her over and over again.

Swallowing thickly, I direct Elwis toward the slope where the grass meets the lake. She obliges, treading carefully along the sharp descent to the water's edge.

Without taking my eyes away from the ruins of this once magnificent kingdom, I dismount Elwis, pulling the reins over her head. My gaze shifts to the main bridge, which is shockingly semi-intact. I brush my hand beneath Elwis's mane.

"Wait here."

She whinnies in response.

I take off at a jog, halting before the remains of the long wooden bridge. Before the racai brought this kingdom to its knees, this path was the only way into the city, save for swimming or sailing.

I hop onto the first set of planks, and a high-pitched creak resonates from their waning wood. Unwilling to test its limits, I hop onto the next cluster of intact planks, then the next, then the next. I continue down the bridge, leaping from one set of wood to the next until finally, I reach the city. Few bridges remain unbroken, and for those remaining whole, the edges of their wood are blackened and charred. Untrustworthy.

I survey the rubble that circles me, plotting a path in my mind. Cautiously, I leap onto another set of planks. They bow beneath my weight, and I prepare to leap onto the remains of the structure before me, but the wood gives out before I can make it, and I land hard on my stomach, the wind knocked from my lungs. I suck in a sharp breath, using my hand to push myself up, away from the sharp, sandy stone digging into my abdomen. A grunt rises in my throat, and I climb through the rubble, my stomach throbbing from the contact. I bite back sudden nausea, gripping my abdomen. When I am able to find an even slab of rock, I straighten my posture, gritting my teeth against the throbbing pain.

I take a few steadying breaths, eyes roving the space around me. Gentle waves lap at the edges of the beige stone, washing over the stray planks and eroding their edges.

Why am I here?

Why is it I have decided to climb into the rubble of this fallen city? There is nothing I seek here.

There will be no survivors, not in a carnage such as this.

Not in a battle such as the one they fought, in a city suspended in the centre of a lake, caught between a burning kingdom and the blades of their enemies, whilst a storm raged above them. It is a miracle Thalia and I escaped.

So what draws me here, I do not know, yet I continue to move through the debris, hopping from one place to another, avoiding the cool waters.

When I reach the palace, I pick through its wreckage, searching for what, I do not know. Signs that somebody made it out? Signs that not everybody perished in that battle?

A body?

I do not know, but whatever compels me, I do not try to tamp it down. I continue to search the carnage, leaping from one sandy-coloured stone to another. Shattered glass is strewn through the wreckage, much of it from the decorative windows, stained in bright colours that now reflect the sunlight, casting blues and purples and greens over the debris. Despite their beauty, they make finding a safe path all the more difficult. At one point, I stumble across a scorched tapestry. I recognise it as hanging from one of the corridor walls.

I lower myself into a crouch, resting one arm on my knee as I lift the fabric. Its once brilliant, shimmering gold is now blackened, scorched. I swallow, dropping it.

Bringing myself to stand once more, I turn in a slow circle, examining the fallen palace around me. There is nothing here.

No trace of life nor death.

No sign of survivors.

There is nothing but rubble.

I do not know what I had been thinking, for I knew from the beginning, from the moment we left this burning kingdom, that nobody would leave alive.

I suppose a part of me had been clinging to that hope, no matter how foolish or irrational.

I had clung onto it for the people of this kingdom, for Calivar.

For Thalia.

Turning, I begin to make my way back towards the bridge, to the shore where Elwis awaits my return.

A glimmer catches my eye.

I halt abruptly, pivoting to the side, where a shimmer of blue, caught beneath a heavy boulder, grasps my attention. My eyebrows draw together as I lower myself into a crouch, placing one hand against the cold stone to support myself as I inspect the object.

A gemstone.

Two of them.

They are small, and what was once carved into a perfect circle is now slightly chipped, jagged. These gems were once a symbol of this kingdom, inlaid throughout, set above the entranceway and various places within the village and palace.

I slip my hand between the boulder and the coarse wood beneath, digging the stones out of the wreckage, despite their resistance. Their surface is cool to the touch, and I catch them against my palm, yet as I begin to draw my hand free, my fingers catch on to something else.

Something cold, solid. I latch my finger around it, guiding it free.

I collapse against one of the boulders, drawing one knee to my chest as I examine my findings. The blue gems are barely the size of my thumbnail, and I slip them into my pocket, turning my attention to the remaining object.

A necklace.

It is gold, the chain thin yet smooth. I trail my fingers over the cool gold, catching the charm in my palm.

It is a locket carved into the shape of a heart.

Upon its surface, a heliotrope is engraved. Gently, I brush my thumb over the embellishment, studying its carefully intricate design. It is hand carved, and by the tiny, intricate details, I suspect it was done by the giver.

Delicately, I open the locket.

*Meria.*

My heartbeat falters.

My breathing slows as I stare at the locket in my hand, at the name written on this frail piece of paper. At the man it is signed by, a small heart inked beside the word.

Thalia's father.

And it is addressed to her mother.

A lump forms in my throat, grief coiling in the pit of my stomach, rising to my chest and weighing me down. My heart throbs painfully, and I drop my head, closing my eyes as my fingers close gently over the locket, securing it within my grasp.

For a while, I sit there, lost in my thoughts and a wave of endless sorrow.

A sorrow for Thalia, for all the tragedy and heartache she has endured.

A sorrow that is not for Thalia alone but for her parents. For what they, too, endured.

I sit for a moment, forcing myself to swallow the lump in my throat and steady my breathing to calm the war of emotions raging within my chest. After a while, I raise my head, blinking the tears from my eyes. As my vision clears, my gaze dips to the debris where I had pulled the necklace from, and I tilt my head at another loose object, which must have come free when I found the locket. It is a golden key, woven at the top into flowers, small hearts set between each, and in the centre, there is a tiny flower, perfectly preserved and only slightly faded. Its centre is a pure white, dappled with purple streaks, then fading into a lavender pink.

Alstroemeria.

A layer of gold traces its outside, following the flower's shape in a protective case. I reach for it, careful as I lay it against my palm and inspect it. The sunlight glances off its surface, making the polished gold shimmer. Not a scratch. Not a pinch of dust.

I have seen nothing like it and hence do not know what it shall open. Nevertheless, I slip both the key and locket into my pocket, where they shall be safely kept.

Then, without another look at the despair that surrounds me, I begin towards the shore once more.

# TWENTY-SIX
## KILLIAN

For the remainder of the day, I continue my journey through the mountains, occasionally feasting upon the small pouch of berries I managed to save. As I begin to near Lsthrain, the need for food is no longer so great, for there, I shall be able to eat to my heart's content, be able to renew my waning energy and nourish myself after these past days.

Yet as night descends, I am forced to make camp in the hills, for I do not wish to reach Lsthrain with no energy. When I arrive, I will not be able to rest immediately, for I am sure there shall be many things I will need to deal with.

My father, for one.

By morning, a portion of my strength has been replenished, and I waste no time descending the mountain, emerging into the vast fields beyond Lsthrain's border.

The tall grass sweeps against my legs, an ocean of colour hidden within their frail strands. Flowers, from heliotropes and gardenias to chrysanthemums, scatter the field, shielded within the towering grasses.

I lean to the side, plucking a red chrysanthemum from the sea of flowers. I twirl its stem gently between my fingers, examining it. Then, I lean forward, twining it into Elwis's mane.

She whinnies in reply, and a soft smile curls my lips.

Although the darkness, the grief, the regret, and the sadness still lingers within my heart, I cannot deny the ever-so-slight sense of joy I feel for returning home.

When I lift my gaze, my eyes snag on the border of the woods ahead, the Forest of Undying Souls. Slowly, I draw my gaze up, where a faint silhouette is visible upon the plateau, backed by mountains.

Lsthrain.

# TWENTY-SEVEN
## THALIA

t takes me merely half a day to reach the field.

Throughout our travels, Alwyne kept a consistent pace, allowing us to arrive in the field just beyond the kingdom's border much earlier than I expected. We had journeyed through the night, for I was too desperate to return to Lsthrain, to aid my kingdom and resolve my argument with Killian to break.

As soon as we break free of the tree line, the sun warms my face, and I tip my head back, enjoying its comfort. An unexpected smile traces my lips, and my grip on the reins loosens.

The tall grasses brush against my legs, tickling my skin through the fabric of my pants. When I open my eyes, I allow my feet to slip out of the stirrups, if only for the short time we shall cross this field, until we reach the border of the undying forest, which is just a short distance away.

It shall be easier to enter Lsthrain from there.

From the corner of my eye, I catch a glimpse of Enia's mountains. I dare not look their way, for I do not wish to diminish this sense of happiness, however tiny.

Alwyne raises his head, mane swishing as he whinnies, and I lower myself so that I am almost flush with his neck, then pat his thick coat.

"You are eager to return, are you not?"

He nickers in response, and a smile curls my lips.

"As am I."

# TWENTY-EIGHT
## THALIA

had forgotten how dark this place was.

It has not been long since I last travelled this forest, yet the events of these most recent days had tamped down the sensation of this forest, for it is nothing compared to the battles I have fought, to the things I have lost.

This forest was only the beginning.

I remember now how it feels.

How the trees blot out every trace of sunlight, how the unease creeps upon you, threatening. It makes the bravest of men flinch at the simplest shift in the air.

I forgot the empty, hollow feeling of it, as if all happiness had been drained from the world. I forgot the way it circles you, taunting, begging you to fall into its false security, promising a life free of pain.

A shiver rakes down my spine, like nails upon a stone slab, and I shudder. Surrounded by memories of the last time I was within the forest, of those I encountered here, I urge Alwyne into a faster pace, eager to be rid of this place.

I am careful to avoid any vines.

A vulture circles above, the flap of its wings vaguely visible through the canopy of trees. As if challenging it, a wolf cries in the distance, followed by a flurry of howls.

I tug on the reins, halting abruptly.

My ears prick, and my eyes rove the surrounding forest, searching the darkness for movement.

A low snarl emits from my side, and I yank the reins, whirling Alwyne to face the wolf.

No, not a wolf.

It is twice the size of a wolf, with a broad, muscular frame. The creature's fur is a rough mixture of light and dark browns. Its eyes are a fierce yellow; its teeth bared, blood-soaked fangs exposed.

Kariyn.

Creatures of Sindir's creation.

The beast edges toward me so slowly it is almost impossible to notice, a skill set they are known for. It maintains eye contact with its prey, inching forward so slowly the victim does not notice until it is too late.

But I notice.

Its growls are low and deep, rising from the base of its throat, and its rugged ears twitch in time with its threats.

This creature believes it may distract me with its beady eyes, force me to give in to my fear and fail to notice its slow edge towards me.

Yet I know better than that.

In one swift motion, my bow is in hand, arrow streaking through the air and piercing the creature through its left eye before it can lunge. It howls, staggering back before dropping dead.

But the kill only draws attention to myself, for I am now surrounded by the rest of its pack.

A lump forms in my throat, but I force it down, carefully raising my chin to appear more intimidating, to boost my own confidence. Slowly, I lift my hand, reaching for another arrow.

But my movement is too unsubtle, and the pack notices.

All at once, they rush Alwyne and me.

I fire my arrow, reaching hastily for another. Following my lead, Alwyne rears, knocking two Kariyn to the ground. Despite their strength and viscous nature, they cannot avoid the rapid firing of my arrows nor the strength of Alwyne's hooves.

Yet I cannot cover every angle, cannot watch my back, which leaves me partly exposed, no matter how hard I try to shield myself.

They do not ignore such an opening.

One of the creatures lunges, knocking me from Alwyne's back.

I land painfully, rolling a couple of times before the oversized wolf pins me down, its sharp, hooked claws digging into my stomach. I bite back a cry as it tears into my skin, and warmth blossoms across my belly.

I struggle against the beast, yet it largely outweighs me and squeezes the breath from my lungs. My arm is limp at my side, the arrow nocked into my bow futile, for I cannot fire it. Its jaw hangs open, revealing rows of pointed fangs covered in the blood of its last victim.

Fear courses through my veins, my heart thudding violently against the inside of my chest.

But I cannot die.

Not when I have a message to deliver, a kingdom to warn.

Not when I have so many things to put right.

My fingers curl tightly about the shaft of my arrow, sliding it free of its nocking point. And as the Kariyn dips its head, saliva dripping from its teeth, I slam the tip of my arrow into its stomach.

It yelps, staggering back off of me, and I grasp my bow, hauling myself into a sitting position. Before it can lunge, I release another arrow, killing it instantly.

Scrambling back, I haul myself onto my feet, pain exploding across my abdomen as I rush to Alwyne and swing myself into the saddle. More beasts sprint towards us, but Alwyne kicks them away as I direct him towards Lsthrain, kicking his sides to urge him on. Dagger now in hand, bow across my back, I lean over, slashing the side of a Kariyn. It yelps, faltering.

Their howls fade as we gallop into the wood.

*

When I am sure the Kariyn are no longer following, I allow Alwyne to slow, granting us the chance to regain our breath.

My hands loosen on the reins, and I find that I am trembling slightly, blood seeping from the wound on my stomach. I look down upon it, where blood stains my skin, circling the shallow yet painful gash upon my belly. Pressing my palm against it, I attempt to stem the flow, and a whimper escapes my lips as a sharp sting echoes through the wound. It is not deep enough for me to bleed out, so it is of minor concern, although the pain is a different matter.

Yet I have nothing to clean it, nothing to wrap it and halt the bleeding. There is nothing I can do but hold my hand against the gash marks, where the Kariyn's claws have sunk into my flesh and wait for the blood to stop flowing.

Only after a while does the bleeding finally stop, and I pull the edges of my blood-soaked shirt over it, concealing it.

My hand is drenched in blood. Features twisting into a grimace as I bend over — the throb worsening — and grasp a leaf to wipe the blood away.

There is no denying my battered state.

The last few days have drained me, not only because of the various injuries I have obtained but the constant battling, the constant travelling and urging myself to stay awake, to keep moving in order to escape my enemies.

The fear, the adrenaline, has drained me.

The sorrow and the pain.

Suddenly, Alwyne raises his head, turning so that his eyes meet mine. He whinnies, the noise echoing through the wood, scaring a flock of birds which erupt from the trees above.

I jolt back to reality, shifting my gaze to follow his line of sight.

Not far into the distance is a break in the trees, where sunlight casts the rugged ground at the base of the tree line in golden light.

Relief washes over me, my heart relaxing as if it were only just released from a fracturing hold.

I am home.

# TWENTY-NINE
## THALIA

I click my tongue, and Alwyne starts forward, towards the border of the forest, his hooves thudding against the rugged ground with newfound determination. Gently tugging on the reins, I bring him to a walk before we emerge from the shadows.

He steps eagerly over a mangled root, and sunlight floods the space before me, casting us in its warm glow.

Joy floods my senses, filling my heart with happiness. It does not feel real to be back, back in this kingdom that I left behind, this kingdom that I grew up in, this kingdom that is my home, in more ways than one. It is a home for my memories, a home for me, and the life I have lived here.

It feels like a dream.

Suddenly, I wish it was.

My heart stutters.

Cracks.

*Shatters.*

No air reaches my lungs.

A strangled gasp parts my lips, and I raise a hand to my mouth, muffling my sudden cry.

The bridge has collapsed.

All that remains is a disfigured stub of cobblestone where the grass ends, dropping to the pond below. The once glistening crystal pond is now filled with jagged pieces of stone, and the bridge has crumbled into its waters.

But it is not only the bridge.

For the entrance has caved in, too.

Where the lookout rests atop Lsthrain's core, its ledge has broken away, collapsed in upon itself, concealing the entrance to my kingdom, forcing the waterfall to flow ruggedly over the sharp boulders, down the cliff face to the ravaged pond below.

That is when I realise I am trembling.

Crying.

Tears stream silently down my cheeks, burning my skin as they mark their path in my flesh.

I shake my head, desperate to believe this is a dream.

A nightmare.

But I know it is not, and I cannot convince myself otherwise.

Desperate, I tap Alwyne's side, leading him to the slope at my right, which leads to the lookout and feast room above what was once Lsthrain's core.

There must be survivors.

There *has* to be.

I lean against his neck as we travel up the steep ascent, tapping his sides as if to speed him up, although I know it makes no difference, for when we crest the top of the slope, the world seems to tilt, my chest growing suddenly heavy as I try to suppress the tears building behind it.

I am too late.

There. Is. Nothing. Left.

No longer is there an open foyer, a short set of stairs leading into the circular room, a corridor curving to the left and into the feast room.

No longer is there the domed feast room, with white stone railings draped with a colourful array of flowers and greenery.

No longer is there the lookout where I would go to be alone, to contemplate and gaze upon the fields, upon Enia's mountains.

No longer is there a canopied well, its intricately carved pillars draped by flourishing vines.

There is nothing but rubble, piles of crumbled stone splattered by the anguishing traces of blood.

Erlys blanket the fallen kingdom, their crystal petals and diamond-like centre seeming to glow against the desolation of this once-flourishing kingdom.

They are a mockery.

A symbol of what we have lost.

But despite the rubble, despite the fallen buildings and the no longer recognisable essence of this place, it is not what breaks my heart the most.

It is the man knelt in the centre of it all, his back to me, chin dropped against his chest, and one hand pressed against the debris. Glistening

Erlys blanket the ground around him, making his despair agonisingly clear.

*Killian.*

# THIRTY
## THALIA

y lips part, and all that emotion, all that pain, comes rushing back to me, crashing in violent waves that threaten to wash me away into a pit of despair.

Without taking my eyes away from him, I slide from Alwyne's back, my limbs trembling as I stand at the crest of the slope, staring at my best friend, the man that has brought me so much happiness and so much pain, knelt in the rubble of his kingdom.

"Killian—"

The word sounds foreign to my ears, and my voice breaks upon it.

Something in him changes then.

His entire body grows rigid, and his head snaps up, pale, honey-blonde hair swaying with the movement.

Slowly, he turns to face me.

And the moment his silver-blue eyes meet mine, I begin to weep. A sob breaks my chest, and I place a hand over my mouth to stifle my cries.

He looks broken.

His entire body is rigid, every muscle in his powerful build strained. The smooth yet sharp features of his face are drawn, pain etched into the arch of his brows, the curve of his lips.

206

His eyes.

His beautiful, striking eyes are filled with a chasm of unending sorrow; their usual silver seemed to have dulled.

He begins to rise, his gaze never leaving mine, never faltering, yet I am already moving towards him, already dropping onto the rubble before him.

He is trembling.

Never before have I seen him like this, so tired, so broken.

"Thalia—" his voice is a whisper, as if my name is unfamiliar on his tongue.

"I am here," I reply gently, tears rushing down my face and scorching my skin. Hesitantly, I take his face between my hands.

His eyes fall closed, long lashes splaying against his smooth skin as he relaxes into my touch. Slowly, I begin to move my thumb back and forth against his cheek.

"I am here," I repeat.

And then I draw him into an embrace, allowing my arms to wrap beneath his, to settle between his shoulder blades and hold him against me. His body sags as if the fight has left him, and his head falls against my shoulder, his silent tears staining the fabric of my cloak. He shifts his position, hands moving to grip my waist.

"I should have killed them all, Thalia. I should have killed the beasts," he says, voice cracking on a sob.

I know not of what he speaks, only that he places the blame on himself when it is not his to bear. Shaking my head, I tighten my hold upon him. "Shh. This is not your fault, Killian. This is not your fault. You did everything you could."

"It was not enough. I should have tried harder—"

"Shh, Killian."

He falls silent, and I squeeze my eyes closed, trying to hold back my tears and be strong for him. But when I can no longer take the pressure building in my chest, I lay my head against his, burying my face in his silky hair.

For a while, we just sit there, knelt in the rubble of what was once our home, our kingdom.

*Killian's* home.

*Killian's* kingdom.

After what seems like an eternity in this place of sorrow, when we can no longer hide from this horrible reality in the warmth of each other's embrace, Killian draws back.

His cheeks are damp, lashes glued together, eyes rimmed with a faint red.

"Thalia, I—" he swallows, throat bobbing.

For a moment, he is silent, struggling against this horrid reality.

"He is not here. I could not find him. I searched, Thalia, I did, yet—" his voice cracks. "My father—"

I nod, closing my eyes once more to stop the tears.

"It is okay, Killian. He is a strong man. They would not have gotten to him so easily. He would—" I halt, carefully phrasing myself.

"Lsthrain is a powerful kingdom. It would not have gone down without a fight, nor would your father. We will find him, I promise."

He drops his chin against his chest, and a single teardrop falls into the mere space between us. I am silent, lips quivering as I watch him, eyes closed, trying to fight this all-consuming pain. His hands are tight on my waist, holding me close, as if he is afraid I shall leave him.

But I will not.

I do not wish to be apart from him again, do not wish to be separated once more. Not now. Not ever.

I do not say a word. Do not coax him into speaking. Do not attempt any words of comfort, for none shall suffice.

For now, I know he wants this silence, needs it.

When he raises his head, his eyes are gleaming, now piercing as ever, and I find myself speechless.

"Are you all right?" I ask softly.

He does not respond.

Does not break my gaze.

There are a thousand thoughts behind his eyes, a thousand emotions and a chasm of pain.

His eyes are their own kind of beautiful, cold when need be, threatening, yet most of the time, they are soft, comforting, able to communicate a thousand things without saying a word.

Over the years, I have learned to read his emotions, his body language and his tone.

His *eyes*.

But here, like this, there is something different behind them, a tenderness I have not seen from him before.

He removes a hand from my waist, lifting it to my face. His knuckles brush against my cheek more gently than I expect. A feather-light touch, as if he is afraid I shall shy away from him.

I do not.

"Are you?" He murmurs.

And for a moment, I just stare into his eyes, searching for an answer, searching for the right words, for an excuse to reassure him that I am fine, to save him from the burden of fretting over me.

But I know it is futile, for we know each other too well.

We can see straight through one another.

Through the truth and the lies.

And I know that nothing I say shall satisfy him, shall tamp down the hurt.

He is suffering, suffering from the loss of his kingdom and his people, from the uncertainty of his father's whereabouts, whether or not he is alive.

And I do not want him to think he is alone.

I do not want him to hurt alone. For if we are to suffer, I would rather we suffer together.

"No," there is a quiver in my voice, a tremble in my limbs and a blurriness in my eyes. I focus on his face, on the sharp curve of his jaw, the arch of his brows and the pain, the concern behind his eyes. The concern as he watches me, the concern for the tears coursing down my cheeks and my heartbreak, even after everything he has been through, and I feel another piece of my heart fall away for this man, who continues to care for me even through his own pain. I focus on the gentleness in his expression, despite everything, on the worry, etched into his features. I focus on the strong hand, now cupping my jaw, the thumb moving in slow, soothing circles against my skin, on the hand that grips my waist, holding me close. "No, I am not."

That is all he needs.

He draws me against him, hand slipping to my back to cradle me against him as I let the tears course down my cheeks. I wrap my arms around his neck, burying my face in its crook as his free hand comes up, resting carefully on the back of my head, fingers tangling gently into my hair as he holds me there, against him. Holds me as I let the pain swallow me. The pain I feel for Killian and his loss, for Ofen losing his childhood home, for all the lives lost and kingdoms fallen, for my own tragedy and heartbreak.

I allow myself to break.

And so does he.

After a moment, he tilts his head, and I feel his damp lashes coast over my skin the moment before his lips brush my temple, and he speaks.

"Nor am I, Thalia. Nor am I."

# ACKNOWLEDGMENTS

I want to write a special thank you to everyone who has helped to make this book more than just words on paper, more than a document on my computer. First of all, a thank you to my parents, who gave me advice and helped me through the stress of juggling my personal, school, and writing life. My mum has been subject to reading through each of my novels to provide me with feedback and ensure nothing coincides or contradicts throughout the trilogy, so thank you, mum. And without my dad, this amazing map would not have been possible. It's safe to say that my skills don't lie with mapmaking. I also want to thank all those who have read and reviewed my book, as well as provided me with comments and feedback, your support means everything to me. Lastly, I would like to thank Atlas Elite Publishing Partners, the people who truly made the publication of my books possible.

Before publishing *Secrets Wrought in Blood,* I was nervous about the publishing process. I did endless research but was still unsure what route I wanted to take. I am beyond grateful that I found Atlas publishing, they made what I thought would be a hard, stressful process into something exciting and worry-free. So, thank you to all those behind the scenes at Atlas, and Michael Beas, for helping me publish my novels. In addition, I want to give a special thank you to Schiammarelly Pinckert Nieme and Dar Dowling. From the beginning, they have been supportive, understanding, and incredibly kind. They have gone out of their way to ensure I am happy with everything.

So a final thank you to my family, friends, and community who have helped me through this. I have begun my journey as an author, and hopefully, one day, I'll be like the writers who have inspired me, who I look up to and dream to be like.

Who knows, maybe my books will end up on a screen.

Manufactured by Amazon.ca
Bolton, ON